JANICE ELLIOTT

The author was born in Derbyshire and has worked as a full-time journalist on *Harper's Bazaar* and *The Sunday Times*. She has reviewed widely, most recently for the *Sunday Telegraph* and has published three highly praised children's books. Of her previous novels, SECRET PLACES was made into a prize-winning film in 1984 with Jenny Agutter, Marie-Theres Relin and Tara MacGowran, THE BUTTER-CUP CHAIN was filmed by Columbia, PRIVATE LIFE was short-listed for the Yorkshire Post Book of the Year, both HEAVEN AND EARTH and THE HONEY TREE were New Fiction Society choices, while the widely acclaimed SECRET PLACES was a Literary Guild choice and won the Southern Arts Award for Literature.

Janice Elliott lives in Cornwall with her husband. She has one son.

sceptre

'Janice Elliott is a smooth operator of enticing fictional stuff. THE ITALIAN LESSON is invisible mending at its most deft, an object lesson in how to knit together a disparate gaggle of Tuscan holidaymakers overtaken by a series of very queer coincidences . . . Janice Elliott has a sharp command of timing and tone'

The Observer

'When a writer as resourceful as Janice Elliott takes it into her head to demonstrate the fickleness of fate, all her characters can do is put their heads in their hands and wait for the thunderbolts to strike. Miss Elliott's admirers will not need to be told that she has a genius for unsettling her readers too'

The Times

'Highly intelligent, rather knowing, a very skilfully-made web of Forsterian motifs ironically elaborated for the 1980s'

New Statesman

'There are some novelists who produce what comes dangerously close to formula fiction and are fêted for it. There are others who offer wide-ranging work of consistently high quality, distinguished by the un-expected, yet who remain outside fashionable acclaim. Such a writer is Janice Elliott . . . THE ITALIAN LESSON sums up all that is good about her work'

Cosmopolitan

Janice Elliott

THE ITALIAN LESSON

Copyright © 1985 by Janice Elliott

First published in Great Britain in 1985 by Hodder and Stoughton Ltd.

Sceptre edition 1987
Second impression 1989

Sceptre is an imprint of Hodder and Stoughton Paperbacks, a division of Hodder and Stoughton Ltd.

British Library C.I.P.

Elliott, Janice
    The Italian lesson.
    I. Title
    823'.914[F]   PR6055.L48

    ISBN 0-340-41239-9

Printed and bound in Great Britain for Hodder and Stoughton Paperbacks, a division of Hodder and Stoughton Ltd., Mill Road, Dunton Green, Sevenoaks, Kent (Editorial Office: 47 Bedford Square, London, WC1B 3DP) by Richard Clay Ltd., Bungay, Suffolk. Photoset by Rowland Phototypesetting Ltd., Bury St Edmunds, Suffolk.

For Jonathan and Joyce Price

THE ITALIAN LESSON

ONE

The first bomb goes off at Heathrow the night before their departure. No one is injured but a crate of soft toys is blown up, dismembering and scattering the remains of teddy bears, elephants, lambs, rabbits, pandas, Wombles and Paddington Bears.

Next morning there is a more than usual edge to the normal anxiety of the thousands (including Fanny and William Farmer) who are processed through the airport. There are few cancellations but many nervy jokes and delays, especially at the machine for scrutinising hand-luggage.

As Fanny says: 'Isn't it crazy – you begin to think there might be explosives in your own handbag.'

William shudders. All his life, even as a child, he has expected accidents, avoided ladders, checked the tide before swimming out of his depth, driven carefully, unplugged the television set in thunderstorms, refused to stroke dogs from Calais south, knowing all the time that the essence of disaster is that it cannot be foreseen. From birth we carry our own death in us. We are fragile. When his children were born he wept for joy and equally for terror at the sight of such vulnerability: the tiny limbs, the thin blue veins too close to the surface of the skin, the skull not yet closed. He was afraid to pick them up in case they broke. When, six months ago, Fanny's baby was stillborn, William wondered even as he brought roses to Fanny's bedside and they clung together in distress, if they had paid their dues to the god of accident, but medically qualified comforters had banished that wild and shocking hope: at Fanny's age, forty-five, the actuarial probability of some such disaster was high. You must not blame yourselves. No one is to blame. So William waits still for the sky to fall. Sometimes he is tempted to seek out the arbitrary fate if only to see its face.

No one knows this about William (though Fanny may suspect it); he is thought of as the soul of reason and that, indeed, is the appearance he presents to the world: the thin, fair-haired Englishman, a type people find reassuring, from whom they expect and get on the whole certain responses. At the polytechnic where he teaches literature in the small unpopular department of liberal studies, he has learned over twenty years to conceal his passion for his subject and to put on a whimsical dryness which evokes from his sullen lumpen students if not respect at least a kind of complicity. It is as though two tribes, alien to each other, had met and agreed not to make the effort to understand one another but to indulge in necessary and relatively peaceful barter: from them the minimal attention by which they might receive the barest facts into their multi-coloured heads; from him the boiling-down of all he holds dear to fleshless bones and passmarks for all who do not use actual violence on each other or the fabric of his classroom. The college is not in any case William's real life. For years he has been secretly writing a monograph on E. M. Forster in Italy: a project of which he has spoken to no one but Fanny, for fear that to speak of it will be to see it dissolve into the thin air whence it came. It is in part the contemplation of this secret that has armoured him against his barbarian students. So he is not afraid of them.

As it happens, William is not particularly afraid of flying either, perhaps because it is something one must do nowadays, as inescapable as crossing the road; also because, once he has surrendered himself to the process, accident is beyond his control.

In fact, everyone feels better after take-off. Once they are above the clouds they are in another zone. They become children again, no longer responsible for this brief period for their destiny. Like children they are told what to do, where to sit, when to fasten and unfasten their seat-belts, when to eat, what to eat, how to suckle the oxygen should the occasion arise. The word emergency is not used. There are even sweets handed round and the colourless nursery food that comes on plastic trays with plastic cutlery and toy pats of butter, and mayonnaise, seal-wrapped.

If, like the Farmers' friend Jay who in his job has been in too many planes in too many time zones, milk is required for an ulcer, milk will be supplied. 'Long Life,' says Jay, meaning the milk and pulls a face as he drinks it obediently from his plastic mug – half a grimace, half a toast.

Lisa, next to Jay, on the other side of the aisle from the Farmers, rummages in her enormous parachute-nylon bag for the toys for her journey: king-size menthol cigarettes, three paperbacks, Yorkie bars, purple knitted slippers, tinted reading spectacles and knitting. Like Jay, she is an experienced traveller. She beams. 'Well, we're off,' she says. 'Hols!'

Fanny smiles. 'I hope San Salvatore will be all right.'

'It's Tuscany. It's bound to be all right.'

Fanny gets the brochure from her handbag. Castello of San Salvatore – not merely a castle but a medieval village rescued from decay by the Marchese of ancient family who gives you now an authentic monument to a vanished way of life. A world untouched since the sixteenth century is yours among the many beautiful walkings of our greeny hills. Delights of our simple cottages and apartments with room for playing children, restaurant commune, hostellerie and culture hall. There is an English page, a German page, a French page and an Italian page, in that order. The spelling of the English page is in American. She has looked at the brochure a hundred times, compared the slight changes of meaning in the different languages so far as she can detect them, and noted that Florence is thirty kilometers only away.

She sighs, puts back the brochure and gets out Gombrich. William has had his nose in a book since take-off.

They are already over the Alps.

Lisa calls across the trolley of Maxpax coffee: 'What is Willy reading?'

Fanny turns to look.

'Forster,' says Fanny.

Lisa nods. Forster. Of course.

William looks up. What are they saying about me? Fanny smiles. She looks happy. She takes his hand and leans across him.

'Look! We're quite low – you can see villages and roads. I didn't know people lived so high up in the Alps. There's a little white car. You can see it quite clearly.'

She is excited. William kisses her. He loves her. He believes in love.

Coming back from the loo Fanny stands aside for the Maxpax trolley on its return journey to the galley and notices the passengers at the forward end of the plane. Two elderly women who look like sisters are sharing tea from a thermos flask. A nun is beaming at a baby a thin girl dressed in jeans and patched smock is holding awkwardly, like a doll. The brown-eyed baby, wrapped in an odd, brightly coloured crochet shawl, grins windily back at the nun and waves its hands. The plane banks abruptly. The seat-belt warning goes on and is delivered verbally in a language that, spasmodically understood, repeats the warning and regrets that in Pisa it is raining.

The nun crosses herself and spells her rosary.

They are going down.

From the little white car Fanny had picked out, Felix Wanderman is conscious of the shadow of the plane before he glances up. From his earthling's view it seems hardly to move, suspended in the sky, so calm, silent and decorous it appears disassociated from the weight, noise and violence of a heavy jet shouldering its unnatural way through the pure air.

For the air up here really is so remarkably clear and refreshing Felix is unaware that above his tonsure of hair (all that is left to him) the sun has polished his pate to a rosy glow which will give him trouble later. With four days of sunshine across France in the open car his weak eyes have troubled him, however, and in Grenoble last night he bought a green eyeshade. While waiting for his change he noticed a model on the cover of *Vogue* sporting an identical piece of gear and was amused. Ada would have told him he looked foolish and doubtless he did but since Ada, to his grief, was not there and would never be there again, sartorial folly seemed unimportant. As he walked from the shop with his purchase Felix reflected that there might be something emblematic about the eyeshade: the first dashing gesture of his widowerhood.

Felix is invigorated in the mountains and reluctant to go down to the plain but he is a fast if eccentric driver and the border arrives sooner than he expects. Here there is a small drama. Where once he need only have shown his passport to be waved through, now on the Italian side he is obliged to climb from his car, his passport is scrutinised and discussed, he is ordered to unlock his boot, to unload his luggage. Perhaps this is the penalty for taking the mountain route out of the busiest tourist season. While they assault his car Felix stands in the midday sun, feeling the heat and wishing he had stopped on the French side for an omelette and a glass of wine in the shade. Even a vermouth and a pizza of Pavia seem infinitely desirable. Although an experienced traveller, he is too dizzy to protest, and perhaps there is some racial, atavistic dread of borders, the fear of being turned back or stranded for ever in the territory between countries where rules may be changed, invented, arbitrarily enforced.

But now they are done, everything is over, Felix has his passport back, they are bored with him. What was it all about? Drugs? Do old men carry heroin in their toilet-bags along with their heart pills, their sleeping pills and their denture cream?

'Bomba,' says the youngest of the customs men who after due empty-seeming contemplation actually helps Felix to close the bonnet. 'Bombs,' he says, 'plastiques. Boom!'

Felix laughs. 'Boom,' he says and they both laugh. The boy, a cheerful young montagnard, is still laughing as Felix puts on his eyeshade and drives off, with a bang and a bump and a wave, until the white beetle car is a wavering speck bouncing down, away, into the cloud.

*   *   *

They had lurched down out of the stratospheric blue through dirty cloud like a child thumping downstairs on its bottom. And now Pisa is a muddle. Pisa is always a muddle, says Jay, smiling his quiet smile. A bulky and ulcerated Ariel, he has circled the globe for twenty years doing whatever it is he does with films, setting them up, talking about setting them up, moving money invisibly and mysteriously across countries, continents, oceans, often with Lisa who has fixed everything or had it fixed so that Jay is by seeming magic in almost perpetual flight. He hardly sees the countries and for him all VIP transit lounges and departure lounges are identical and interchangeable. Except for Pisa, which is hardly an airport at all but a state of mind which some malevolent whim has decided shall be a Clapham Junction of the air where souls in torment must linger before eventually, against all odds, proceeding on their journeys.

So here they are, among other confused and undirected passengers in an inadequate, temporary-seeming building resembling Northolt in the 1940s. And outside it is raining.

William and Jay go to claim the luggage and Lisa to check with the car-rental desk about the Audi (one of the treats of this holiday is the margin of luxury allowed by Jay's expenses: quite legitimate since who knows where on the earth a film might next be set up?). Fanny guards the hand-luggage and, enjoying herself regardless, takes in the scene. The flying nun has been swept up by others of her kind uttering small cries so that in their old-fashioned habits the little group resembles a fluttering gathering of dark birds discussing migration; then all at once they are outside, seen through the glass doors chattering under big black umbrellas which they lower and close almost at once to enter a mini-van with sliding doors. Their wimples are the shape of paper boats and they wag together as they speed away (Fanny remembers the nuns in the convent nursing-home and the fantasy she had of grave beaks bent to peck her as she came round; in fact, they could not have been gentler or more kindly, those sensible virgin women).

The crowd thins but only a little. The elderly English sisters, as Fanny sees them, appear to have detected some emergency and dealt with it smartly. After a discussion – brisk on their side

– with a harassed girl in uniform, they are boarding a Citalia coach.

'I'm sorry – what did you say?'

'I wondered if you knew how to get to Florence?' The fragile girl in smock and jeans, now carrying the baby in a kangaroo sling on her breast (how bad for the shoulders, Fanny thinks) looks as though she might cry. Her brown hair hangs down in sad curtains each side of her face. The baby sleeps. 'You are English, aren't you? You see, the train's on strike.'

'Isn't there a coach? I saw a coach, I'm sure.'

'That's only an airline coach. You have to be with the right airline to get on it. There used to be a coach for everyone but they seem to have cancelled it. I'll have to try and hitch, I suppose,' she says but makes no move, as though she had no strength or will.

'Oh dear.' Fanny feels that the girl has decided she shall be Fanny's problem. People have always done this to her: strangers on trains confide their terminal diseases, those who believe that the world will end next Tuesday jostle aside the Jehovah's Witnesses at Fanny's door, newly met acquaintances at parties cut her off in a corner and present her with their marital problems, their sexual problems, their work problems, their children's excesses, their father-in-law's incontinence; even her children's friends help themselves to food and drink and confession, seeking solace for everything from parental tyranny to herpes. Girls with hair in wild coloured spikes and chipped black nail-varnish, enormous boys (why are they so tall nowadays?) scratching their stubble and blocking out the light (only her own offspring have become secretive, they tell her nothing, she wonders sometimes what happened). Fanny is never required to say anything. They simply dump their lives in her lap and go away feeling better.

The girl is still there. The men have the luggage and Lisa is approaching. She seems worried.

Fanny says: 'Well, I suppose we could give you a lift, if we are going through Florence. Lisa, are we going through Florence?'

'There's been a balls-up. They don't know anything about the Audi. We've got to have a Fiat. There's nothing else.'

'Do we go through Florence? Could we manage one extra?'

'We'll have to go through Florence to get another car. They're all shut up in Pisa. I can't think what Jay will say.'

It is unusual to see Lisa fret. Normally she strides through the world like a girl through a field. But, of course, this is her job, to protect Jay, like a giant baby, from the rubs of life. How indeed could he be kept in almost perpetual motion around the earth without someone to ensure that planes flew, cars arrived on time, hotels and restaurants were booked, meetings set up, beds firm, pillows soft, air-conditioning humming away. Lisa even follows the political news. She may not be able to hold up the planes in the sky, weed out the hijackers or search the hotel basements for bombs but she can at least divert Jay around war zones, of which there is a new one every day.

Fanny grins. 'Lisa, love, we're on holiday.'

And Jay doesn't seem to mind at all: the delay, the rain, the inconvenience of stopping in Florence, the tiny car or the extra passengers. Lisa drives along the excellent road, Jay's great bulk safely lowered into the bucket seat beside her while Fanny, William, the girl called Perry and the baby are squashed less comfortably in the back. But the girl takes up very little space. She seems to have folded herself up to get out of the way as if in the hope that no one will notice she is there at all.

Fanny asks the baby's name.

'Mario.'

'He's very good.'

'Yes, he's lovely.' For the first time the girl smiles and relaxes a little with the baby, holding him more naturally, smiling at him and at Fanny.

'Are you staying in Florence?'

'I'm not sure.'

'We have to get another car there. We're going up into the hills. A place called San Salvatore.'

'Oh, that sounds lovely.'

On the other side William squeezes Fanny's hand. She turns and sees another Fiat, red just like their own, heading in the opposite direction, back towards Pisa. It is being driven too fast and the offside fender is dented.

As they reach the outskirts of Florence the traffic thickens, the rain stops, Jay jerks awake and so does the baby, opening his long-lashed brown eyes in an expression that in an older child would be taken for wonder and delight.

Late that night when Perry has left with a whispered thank-you and Fanny has decided not to worry about her, when a car has been ordered for the morning, they have eaten well, had a night-cap on the Farmers' balcony with the view of Santa Croce, pleasantly dizzy with exhaustion and anticipation and the solemn calling of bells, and gone to their ample beds, an outgoing flight from Pisa to Heathrow is hijacked and diverted to Damascus, where it is turned away and so long as the fuel holds out will continue to fly through the night, charted anxiously by control-towers and governments. No one dare guess which will come first, sanctuary or detonation of the explosive device.

But in their hotel on the Lungarno Fanny and William know nothing of this, for they are asleep, her hand on his arm, his on her thigh. In the adjoining suite Lisa, restored to herself, snores frankly and cheerfully. Only Jay is awake, drinking milk, sprawled in front of the television watching an old Bogart dubbed in Italian. He sighs. Those were the days.

The next morning under a clear blue sky a number of vehicles are making their way up the road from Florence through San Domenico and Fiesole. Although the Audi is the faster car Felix Wanderman is an earlier riser than the Farmers and their friends, so they do not meet the white open-topped beetle until they are nearly at Fiesole. Here Jay, misjudging a blind corner, pulls out to overtake the smaller car with the GB plate. With the bus from Florence on his heels, it is too late to drop back when there appears on the opposite side of the narrow road a coach carrying German art historians down the hill to the European University. Felix has been watching his mirror and whips to the right into a private driveway, allowing Jay a free passage. An accident has been averted. Jay waves his thanks and Fanny, in the nearside seat, catches a glimpse of a man with a fringe of grey hair round a bald pate, mopping his brow. In the bus from Florence two elderly Englishwomen who are not actually sisters but have been travelling together for many years, observe the near-collision and let out a little puff of relief that there is to be no emergency or Italian confusion or blood, drama and road strewn with bodies. They are particularly glad the small car with the British plate has not been squashed, for in a meeting of large car, coach and bus, it would certainly have been the loser.

The owner of the villa in whose driveway Felix pauses for a moment to collect himself is unaware of any drama outside her high walls, screening ilex, conifer and eucalyptus. A little bundle of bones clad in green silk pyjamas, propped against soft cushions on her terrace, old Daisy Pottinger waits for her maid to rub almond oil into her pink scalp and meanwhile peels a nectarine, wondering if anything will ever happen again.

TWO

'Bliss,' says Lisa, 'isn't it?' She peels a peach ready for Jay but bites into hers whole, skin and all. Now they are arrived and sterilised milk has proved available for Jay and his bed firm enough and pillows soft enough and there have been no accidents and Lisa, William and Fanny are breakfasting on the terrace that joins the Farmers' one-floor apartment to Jay's casa, Lisa has relaxed at last. She wears her thick grey-blonde hair in a plait down her back, a long dun-brown cotton skirt, vast sweater with sheep walking round it (the morning air is from the Apennines, brilliant and cold) and a necklace of what appear to be dried fruit stones and miniature gourds.

Although they have known each other for many years this is the first holiday the friends have taken together and Fanny is intrigued by Jay's and Lisa's domestic arrangements.

'Well, do they or don't they?' Fanny murmured last night as she and William sat propped on their bed sharing duty-free Scotch.

'Mm? Do they what?'

'You know. I mean are they?'

William looked at his cigarette. It would probably give him lung cancer or heart disease. But then if you gave up having been accustomed to it for many years, Obesity and Stress pounced with a Coronary, while deeper in the forest lurked Alcoholism and Addiction to tranquillisers. It was swings and roundabouts.

'Lisa does and he doesn't.'

'Really?' Fanny even after all these years was startled by the decisiveness and frequently the accuracy of William's judgements. It is as though the dormouse had raised his head from the teapot and uttered a definitive declaration on Keynesian economics.

'Have you known this all the time?'

'Yes.'

'Why didn't you say?'

'You never asked.'

Fanny took a deep breath.

'I'm sorry we don't much at the moment either. Make love, I mean. Perhaps Italy will change that. It does change things, doesn't it.' Her tone was wistful.

William stubbed out his cigarette.

'It doesn't matter. I love you.'

Fanny smiled. 'I know.'

She did too, but all the same when Willy had slipped into a doze she went to the window and looking out at the view – the dusty-red tiled roofs, the fortified walls, the sentinel cypresses, the lights of Fiesole and further still, down, the stream of stars that was Florence – she thought the gods are still here, warming the earth, all will be well again, I shall be healed.

Already this first morning they are looking for something to do. The sky-blue Audi slumbers in the medieval car-park. They have only just had their breakfast and they are in varying degrees restless. The speed of air travel (barring accidents) means that those who are by temperament or conditioning bad at doing nothing have no chance to shrug off their natural busyness. They insure themselves before leaving not only against accident but idleness. Jay and Lisa have film-scripts, Fanny a secret intention to take up painting where she left it at evening classes when the children were small and the only time she was not housebound was when William came home at seven. (After the first and only au pair had an accident with the Volvo and might have killed the children had they been riding with her at the time, Fanny took over their care entirely and found she relished their infancy more than anything that had happened to her before or since.) She will also try to learn a little more Italian than the basic exchanges of which she is capable from earlier holidays in

Venice and in the Argentario. Even William, who could never be
mistaken for a whizzer, has plans.

Still all tell themselves and each other that they are open to
other options. In fact they are keen. The Middle Ages, the
pre-Renaissance and the Renaissance lie all around and below,
theirs for the taking. Rome speaks from the stones, Etruscan
graves with narrow entrances yawn beneath their feet.

It is, in a way, too much, which explains perhaps why they
have chosen San Salvatore. Here is a world complete in itself,
a structure, somewhere to tell them what to do. Start here
then. The rest can wait.

'Oh Jay,' says Lisa, 'there was an Antonioni season in the
cinema last month! We've missed it. This newsletter's out of
date.'

Fanny knows she must not catch William's eye or she will
giggle. Though to her credit Lisa too sees the joke as soon as
she has spoken.

'Oh Lordy, sorry.'

Jay laughs. He has an immensely comforting laugh. He is not
an ugly fat man. There is something both vulnerable and lovable
about his bulk. Give me fat men about me, thinks Fanny with a
pang of disloyalty; recalling William's pronouncement on the sex
lives of Jay and Lisa she glances at the two of them and realises
as clearly as if it had been spoken aloud at that moment, yes,
of course, he's right. (Lisa has never discussed her liaisons at
any length but there is a memory of her with her wide grin after
a couple of large brandies: 'I'm a nympho, you see' – a remark
dismissed with laughter, now surfacing in Fanny's mind as she
takes in this morning's picture of Lisa, wide thighs spread,
tipping her face back to the sun as she pulls grapes from a bunch
with her teeth. What other revelations will this holiday bring?
Fanny wonders.)

'Well, does anyone want to go anywhere?' Fanny asks.
'Florence or Fiesole? San Domenico?'

Oh no, they say, not today, too tired. Let's find out what's
happening here. Who wants to be a tripper?

'I do, quite,' says William, then puts his head back in the
teapot.

'In that case,' says Fanny, 'we ought to ask at that reception place. Where is reception?'

They spread on the table the map of the Castello that came with the brochure and Fanny and Lisa bend over it glancing up to relate the flat map to the three-dimensional reality. It is as fascinating as those children's pop-up picture books. There is the only modern building – the circular conference hall – there the central winding street, at the top the albergo, at the bottom the restaurant, the walled gardens entered through iron gates, the playground with swings and slides. They cannot see the discreetly screened car-park but outside the walls, between the Castello and the wooded hill, is the area marked on the map with a wigwam – a camp-site for students with facilities for cooking and washing. Above the site is a cleared area of flat brown grass upon which at that moment a yellow helicopter is landing, the first sign of movement they have seen that day.

Now they look again the landscape seems to have woken up. While two passengers leave the helicopter, making for a tower drawn but unmarked on the map, and the helicopter at once takes off again, a small white car is making its way up the road from Fiesole, panting, it appears, with the effort, and playing hide-and-seek with the watchers as it weaves along the circuitous tree-lined route. Two doll-sized figures are approaching the reception hall, coming up from one of the lower apartments near the gatehouse.

'Come on,' says Lisa. 'Let's go.'

'Ferdinando,' says the amiable young man behind the reception desk in the large hall which must once have been grim but now – painted white with a modern window giving on to a vertiginous view, like a travel poster for holidays in Italy – has the air of a not unpleasant waiting-room in which people sit on marble benches studying guide-books and brochures or read the numerous notice-boards that line the walls.

'I'm sorry?' Fanny wonders if she had missed something vital. A password? Willy has wandered off and is reading notices. Jay sits.

'My name is Ferdinando. I shall be pleased to service you at any time.'

'Wow,' says Lisa behind her hand.

'Farmer,' says Fanny. 'We got our keys at the gatehouse last night.'

The serviceable young man consults his register.

'Ah. Yes. Michelangelo and Bronzino. The names of your apartments,' he explains. 'You are happy?'

'Yes, thank you. That is, we would like a programme of activities.'

'Here,' he says, bringing out a sheaf of xeroxed papers. 'And there,' pointing to the notice-boards. 'Have a good day. I like America.' And turns away to attend to a new arrival, a short, elderly man in spectacles surrounded by old-fashioned baggage. As he bends slightly Fanny observes a tonsure of greyish hair surrounding a pate that appears to have been rather dreadfully sunburned.

'Yes, of course. I saw you on the plane.' William has been talking to two elderly Englishwomen who might be sisters. Fanny, joining them, finds something pleasing in the meeting of travellers who were strangers and have – somehow magically it appears to her – converged at the same destination. They are not sisters, it seems. Their names are Miss Stimpson and Miss Head. This they reveal as they stroll with the Farmers up the hill from the reception hall to the miniature central square with fountain and bar. (Lisa and Jay have stayed behind to book for the Buñuel film that night or it might be the Vivaldi concert. Fanny hopes it might be Vivaldi.) Miss Stimpson, or it might be Miss Head, is the taller and wears orthopaedic sandals, a woven cotton skirt with a vaguely Greek frieze pattern around the hem, a large floppy sunhat tied under the chin and the look of a Saluki dog or Virginia Woolf as an interesting horse. When she smiles her blue eyes are pretty. Miss Head, or it might be Miss Stimpson, is shorter and ready for anything in a Windsmoor skirt, sturdy shoes and ankle socks and a practical khaki bush hat – Israeli army style – jammed so firmly on to her skull she might have no hair at all. Both carry walking-sticks, the Saluki-lady's interestingly reminiscent of a shepherd's crook.

'And then on the Citalia coach. You were lucky.'

'Oh yes,' says the shorter (Miss Head) as they pause at the crossroads, 'one gets to know the tricks. Didn't we see you on the road to Fiesole? Near the Villa Inglese?'

'Oh dear, yes. You mean you were on the bus?' Fanny wishes William would say something. He was talking enough before she arrived.

'We thought you were Italian. They drive wildly but not as badly as the Belgians. Odd about the Belgians, don't you think?'

'It was a hire-car, you see.'

'We always get the bus to Fiesole, don't we, Win?'

Mrs Woolf-Stimpson smiles with her pretty eyes.

'And then we have to have a taxi but we've got a man in Fiesole who always takes us, Cissie found him years ago. She always knows the ropes. Such a relief. So hot otherwise, don't you think?'

Oh yes, it was very hot. But Italy was worth it. Of course. Always. Miss Stimpson runs on, a shy stream undammed. No, thank you, very kind, lovely, but they won't stop, a little hike up for the view. When you get to the top of the hill there's always another, isn't there. A picnic in our packs and a funghi-hunt. A flutter of a hand on William's arm. We'll see you quite soon then, don't forget.

There is something touching about them Fanny thinks, and brave; and then she thinks I am patronising, they are people, women, travellers like us, no more, no less.

'What are they hunting? I wouldn't have thought they were blood-sports.'

William laughs and kisses her, there in the middle of the square in the midday sun, mouth upon mouth.

'Mushrooms,' he says. 'It's the mushroom season.'

'You're very chipper.'

'Chipper. That's a funny word, isn't it. Where did you get that from?'

Fanny giggles and says it again. Chipper.

There are Lisa and Jay coming up the hill from reception, arm in arm. Heavy weather for Jay.

The sun is directly overhead. They sit in the shade of the bar awning, drinking vermouth, except for Jay and his Perrier. William sups from Fanny's glass and then swops her white for his red. What's he up to?

They drink and discuss what has happened so far and what will happen.

Lisa says: 'That gorgeous creature at reception! Isn't he priceless. Wherever did he spring from?'

'Gorgeous?'

Fanny glances at Lisa. She looks like someone contemplating a particularly delicious meal. Now the matter has come up she finds herself viewing her friend with fresh and widened eyes.

Innocently, William offers: 'He's supposed to be an illegitimate sprig of the Marchese's. Apparently he really is very helpful. You know, hot-water bottles and things.'

They are startled. 'Willy, how do you know?'

'Stead and Simpson. They've been here before.'

'Stead and – ? Oh, Willy's made a joke!' Lisa pecks his cheek.

William smiles modestly.

'You seem to have had quite a chat with them. What else did you talk about?'

William leans back, rather enjoying himself.

'Oh, places to go. How to get there. You know, this and that. Florence. Forster.'

'*Forster?*'

He nods. 'They've got a little study group here at the moment. At teatime in the garden.'

Lisa is dumbfounded. 'You mean you've come to Tuscany to drink tea and talk about Forster?'

'Oh, not exclusively. But I'll keep my eye open. I don't suppose we'll find the Pensione Simi. I gather though there's a villa near Fiesole – one of those places the English used to gather. If the woman's still alive she might remember something.

But it's more the spirit of the place. It's still here, don't you think?'

Jay shakes his head.

'You'd have to go a long way to find Forster's Italy now. It's a museum. This place is a museum.'

Lisa taps William's hand.

'You know, I believe our Willy's a closet romantic. Come on. Confess.'

'If it's romantic to believe in love and tolerance, yes.'

Fanny changes the subject. A coach has drawn into the car-park and a party of trippers, wearing assorted funny hats, with burned knees and noses, is making its way up towards the square.

'Time for lunch. Then we'll settle what to do.'

Following Lisa and Jay back to the casa, Fanny catches William's arm and they pause. 'Look,' she says, and there below the Castello and the trippers, close against the fortified walls, is a grey olive grove they have not noticed before. Love? she wonders. Tolerance? A spirit in the grove? There's someone there now, a shape, an animal, a man, resting in the shade of the dry leaves and twisted limbs. In spite of the trippers she and William are held in the absolute stillness of midday, the mezzogiorno. From a campanile somewhere below, Fiesole perhaps, a bell reminds: wait, be still, and another – or it may be the echo – answers, I am, I shall. Fanny thinks of the peace above the clouds, the secret bombs around the world, on the earth and in the air, William's accidents, the lost girl and the beautiful baby, her own loss, Mr Forster, and Lucy Honeychurch in Santa Croce without a Baedeker, Florence spread for them there in the plain below; and she feels a fierce protectiveness for William and a wish to believe so powerful she opens her mouth to speak. When a military jet which will crash tomorrow in the high snows of the Apennines, rips the sky apart and stuns the earth.

In the grove the jet wakes Felix Wanderman from a doze. Immediately on arrival this morning he parked his no longer white but sadly grey beetle next to the vaguely familiar blue

Audi, registered, asked for his bags to be sent to his room (no porters, of course, but age has its benefits still at least in Italy, at least sometimes) and made straight for the tempting shade of the grove he had glimpsed on the last turning in the road. The rain from the border to Florence, the uncomfortable night in Florence with a sick headache from the sunburned head and the near-accident on the road that in his already exhausted state had shaken him badly and compelled him to spend an even more uncomfortable night at Fiesole, had left him hungry for greenness and silence.

What an extraordinary chance it had been that swerving to save the undeserving Audi, he had found himself, dizzy and panting, at the gate of the Villa Inglese. Almost he had pulled the bell but the place looked overgrown and there could be little chance that old Daisy was still alive, or if she were alive that she would recognise him, or if she recognised him that she would be pleased to see him. Perhaps a little later when the mood took him, he would find out. Meanwhile at the thought of Daisy he smiled. Too many funerals nowadays, a sense of dread when he turned to the obituaries that frequently spoiled his breakfast. Everyone falling off their perches – it was a relief to read of the few who had gone not after illness bravely borne but snatched by accident. With age the aspiration to die in one's bed loses its charm, the bolt from the blue grows increasingly enchanting. Bomba! Boom!

But of Daisy's death he has not heard, so although reasonably she must be dead, it was possible to remember her happily, alive. And he had so nearly had his bolt from the blue at her gate. That would have tickled her and it would have been in a way orderly: life describing a circle, returning like a vapour trail in the sky to cross its own path.

But Felix had not died at Daisy's gate. He is alive, sore-headed and, having identified his room on the map, is sitting on his bed. He regains his breath, wipes his spectacles and takes in his room. White-painted, tiled floor with simple mat, chair, desk, wooden bed, it is spotless enough for a hospital. Well, he has been in worse rooms in his time and here, after all, is everything he needs. And he has learned long ago that a traveller alone

cannot expect the bridal suite. Such as he are never popular
with hotels which is largely why he has chosen San Salvatore.
Not that luxury has ever been to his taste. At home he lives in
a cave of disordered and dusty books, any one of which he could
lay his hand on at once with the instinct of the blind mole he
resembles.

Ada, he thinks. When she was alive and travelled with him
she had the gift of making a home at once in any of their
temporary lodgings. A shawl, one of the dolls she collected from
all over the world, her musky scent, a little carved African figure
she cherished: these lares and penates transformed the meanest
room.

Enough of that! For grief there is always another time.
Unpack. Books first on the table (a more than adequate reading
light for once). Clothes: of little importance. You could never
make me into a dandy, could you Ada, my love? So now it is
drip-dry shirts that prickle the skin, a dinner jacket with a bloom
of verdigris; the only folly a bow-tie bought in New York that
Ada had considered vulgar. Free to wear it now, flaunt it if he
wishes. Perhaps he will.

In the bathroom Felix sets out his shaving materials (old-
fashioned cut-throat razor) and the pills that are supposed to
keep him alive, heart pumping correctly, arthritis under control.
Pretty sweets for sleeping and waking and hope. Sometimes he
takes them, sometimes he does not. With a glint in his eye he
decides to do without and although in a week he may pay the
price, at least he will enjoy for that time an illusion that he alone
controls his destiny. (He is also aware that in this pharmacopoeia
he carries the means of ending his life and more than once in
the year since Ada's death he has counted out the necessary
number. What makes him hold on after all? Felix wonders.
Work, he supposes. And curiosity: that is the last instinct to
survive, the saving urge.)

Felix puts on his carpet slippers and unknots his tie. Before
lunch he will rest. It is true that he is tired and his heart
crashes. First though he remembers and returns to the bathroom, tipping his head to inspect. He reaches for the bottle
of calamine lotion and the cotton wool he bought yesterday

in Fiesole and anoints his rosy pate until it looks like a white eggshell.

In the middle of the afternoon Fanny wakes from a sleep at once deep and alarming to find William missing from the bed. Of course, Willy is talking about Forster with the old ladies in the garden.

From now on, when the trippers are banished at four o'clock, everyone in San Salvatore seems to be talking or listening or asking or telling or debating, or discussing what they will say or listen to or watch or hear. It is safe now. The armies of chaos, following the tracks of the Medicis, have failed to sack the Castello and retreated down the mountain to Florence, their proper place, to gasp on their beds, complain that they cannot open the shutters because of the mosquitoes and they cannot breathe because the air-conditioning has broken down. (At least the mosquitoes are – one trusts – no longer malarial.) And then they will rise from their beds and go in search of that delicious Italian food that is somehow never as delicious as you expect. And send postcards home showing the muddy brown Arno quite brilliantly blue.

At San Salvatore there are no such problems. Or rather, there are (mosquitoes, for instance, though not too many at this time of year) but the expectations are those not of the tripper but of the serious visitor to Italy or of the kind of person who has long ago digested Italy and simply finds this a quiet and pleasant spot. Academics on sabbatical, old Italian hands like the Misses Stimpson and Head, scholars like Felix Wanderman wanting to work and play a little, novelists after nervous breakdowns, quietly spoken Americans from expensive but unostentatious clapboard houses in Connecticut, specialists in high-Renaissance church music, novelists with blocks, internationally known continental film-makers, cellists with broken wrists, novelists with lovers (who can tell their wives they are attending cultural conferences), critics with exhausted spleen, or people like the Farmers, Jay and Lisa who are simply tired of hotels and rented farmhouses in the Dordogne – all can be sure of finding at San Salvatore (personal introduction essential, no advertisements) people of their own kind and diversions to their taste. Even the lack of luxury is attractive. The white-washed rooms, the spare but pleasing country furniture, the unpretentious refectory restaurant, appeal to those discovering here an oasis of simplicity in their over-busy lives. Most do not bring children but those who do may dispatch them to the playground with its small pool and climbing frames designed by the sculptor in wood who has recently had such a success with his outdoor exhibition at the Forte di Belvedere. There is even a crèche where mothers may deposit their offspring for an hour or two and run off to play with light hearts, for it is well known that Italians love babies.

At the little bar in the corner of the restaurant the Misses Stimpson and Head, back from their funghi-hunt, having skipped their siesta for the sake of Mr Forster, are drinking Perrier with lemon slices and recommend the seminar on Giotto if one is to know what one is looking at, though of course one must not take these things too seriously; for the true Italy one must tramp about a bit and ride on buses. No, at this time of year they do not feel the need for a nap and if the weather holds Monteverdi in the upper gardens tonight would be delightful. They are having an early supper. Their mushrooms are being cooked for them now, you can smell them, can't you?

Fanny smiles. 'So your hunt was successful?'

'Oh yes! Full baskets!' Miss Head beams back. 'But Win was silly and went without socks. It was quite a nasty gash from the brambles but your husband was so kind. Just the man to have around in case of accident.'

Win blushes. Lisa looks as though she might giggle. Fanny is puzzled. William gazes modestly into his glass.

'Kind?'

'We'd washed it, of course, but he took one look and went for the iodine.'

'Oh yes.' Fanny understands. 'William always travels with a full medicine cabinet.' Even to cross the road, she thinks and then repents. It must be terrible to live like Willy.

Lisa, who was on the edge of wickedness, has decided to

behave. William is fetching more drinks and in the pause, so to speak, in the action, the attenuated Miss Stimpson (whose hair without the floppy sunhat is revealed as quite pretty, somewhere between grey and soft brown, bundled on top of her head into a mouse-nest heap from which soft tendrils escape) takes a wild plunge and dips her flamingo-neck in Lisa's direction.

'Such a pity, isn't it, about I Tatti?'

'Is it?'

'That it's closed? Berenson, you know, at Settignano; it must have been fun. We saw him once. He was eighty-three in 1950.'

Lisa gives the shy lady her best grin.

'I'm afraid I don't know. I don't know very much at all actually.'

'Oh, surely you do.'

'Only movies.'

'Oh dear. We don't get to the cinema very often, do we Cissie? I know we should. Though we like the old films on television. Sometimes.'

Miss Head downs her glass and addresses Fanny.

'We were telling your husband about the Villa Inglese. If he wants to get in I should ask Ferdinando. He can fix most things. Ah, there you are, Mr Farmer. I was telling your wife you should ask Ferdinando at reception about the Villa Inglese. If you're still interested.'

'Very interested. Thank you.'

Miss Head nods. 'Come on, Win, I can see our mushrooms coming up.'

Lisa lets out a long snort.

'Aren't they priceless?'

Fanny says: 'I think they're rather sweet. Did you enjoy your Forster tea with them, Willy?'

'Oh yes. I did. I enjoyed it quite a lot.'

Lisa is hungry. 'That smell is driving me mad.'

'Then let's eat.'

'What?' says Jay, who has been studying the menu, hand-written on a child's slate, with a gentle sadness.

Lisa looks at the menu and at Jay's face.

'Cheer up. We'll find something. Mushrooms are all right, aren't they?'

'What about the garlic?'

'No garlic, we'll tell them, absolutely no garlic. What's the Italian for garlic?'

Fanny shakes her head. Lisa takes the menu from Jay and kisses him on the cheek. He is smiling again. Friends, thinks Fanny – when all the rest is gone, nothing like friends.

Fanny thinks, sitting at one of the two long scrubbed refectory tables, the restaurant might qualify as pretentiously unpretentious. A sort of nursery game in which everyone is playing grown-ups in a restaurant is how the scene strikes her. The internationally known continental film director allows a girl who resembles remarkably the Farmers' ex-au pair to tuck his napkin under his chin and to feed him with a fork from the dish of antipasto set before each place. At the far end of their own table she notices the only person who looks entirely comfortable on the bench vacated by medieval monks who must have had short legs – the elderly tonsured man who had been in reception this morning. Since she can see the top of his head (which seems oddly familiar) he cannot be more than five feet tall or so. He wears a rather astonishing red-spotted bow-tie and reads from a book propped up against a carafe, while he spears his antipasto. He has the air of someone who has been here before and is not to be distracted by the goings-on, the shrieks of greeting, the kissings, the chatter, the somehow desperate attempts on the part of each band of newcomers to make it clear that they are at home here, they know their way around.

Fanny is reminded of birthday parties for her children, Alison and Robin, when they were small: the near-hysterical anticipation, the too-bright eyes, over-eating and ritual crashing and smashing as games got out of hand and ended in tears, in one infant at least being sick or howling when he failed to win the prize. The birthday child, in particular, would always finish the afternoon tremulous with unfulfilled expectation. At the time Fanny thought, she told herself, she enjoyed doing this for her children, recalling hazily the ceremonies of her own childhood. It strikes her now how she hated every minute of the whole business, resenting both Willy's absence and the innocence of his return at the end of the day, bearing presents they could not afford; so the one whose birthday it wasn't grew querulous again and the other frenzied.

And then no present, Fanny remembers, ever satisfied. But in fairness perhaps that is always true? We all await the divine ultimate gift, the chalice, the golden bowl that will irradiate and transform our lives and it never arrives, in anything but anticipation. There is some deeper consideration here, about her children and how she had longed for them and now in the vague and ever-present sadness at their estrangement has made a shrine in her mind of their childhood in which they are always small and sweet and she sits with them in the clearing in the long grass and loves them with an immediacy she has known in no other relationship. Is that what she misses, their imagined childhood? What she was seeking to recover with the one that was lost? It is extraordinary how clearly she sees that one, the boy, though she never saw him; in dreams he calls to her as though he had been abandoned and she wakes in tears.

But this is why she is in Italy – to get over the dreams, to bury him once and for all.

'What? Sorry?'

'Hey, Fanny, where are you?' Lisa is watching her closely. 'What d'you want to eat? Mushrooms or mushrooms?'

'Oh. Whatever. Mushrooms I suppose.'

The slate bearing the chalked menu of the day has been passed down the table and Lisa has put on her giant owl spectacles to read it.

'Apparently you can choose afterwards but you have to have mushrooms first – like bread and butter before jelly.'

'Oh, I am sorry,' Fanny says across the table to Stead and Simpson who have just finished their mushrooms. 'You needn't have bothered hunting.'

'The fun of the chase,' says Miss Head.

'But it says Ovoli here.'

'That's the Amanita caesarea – the fungus the Romans favoured. Trippati's best, almost a meal in itself. Fabrizio does them beautifully sautéd, then covered with sauce and parmesan.'

'Yum,' says Lisa.

'Can you get them plain grilled?' Jay wonders.

'Tell Fabrizio gratella,' says Miss Head.

Fabrizio appears to be both host and cook. He wears a butcher's striped apron over white canvas trousers and white silk polo-necked shirt. He is clearly an autocrat whose favour is much sought. As he patrols his territory he pauses now and then at one group of diners or another and immediately the buzz of excitement increases. The most favoured females are even permitted to kiss him on each cheek. He is not interested in the Farmers. It is an underling who takes their order and makes no attempt to conceal his impatience as Lisa struggles to convey on Jay's behalf that the signore wishes simply the mushrooms and a little milk if that is possible. It is only Miss Head's intervention that saves the day.

'I'm afraid Fabrizio bullies him rather. Well, come on Win. Our constitutional then up the wooden hill. We're early birds,' she explains.

Lisa is torn between hunger and haste.

'We'll have to get a move on. The film starts at nine.'

'Oh, it's the film is it?' Fanny is finding the Chianti too sharp but then she always says wine is wasted on her: the ones she really likes remind her of Ribena.

'We were lucky to get tickets.'

William wonders vaguely if they have come to Italy to go to the cinema but he is in a good mood, something about today has put him for the moment to rights with the world. He has permitted himself – in a mild way – to enjoy today.

'All right, love?' he says.

Fanny smiles. 'Fine. I'm fine.'

She swallows the wine without tasting – that's better. Now Stead and Simpson have gone she can ask Willy.

'Whatever did you talk about at your Forster tea?'

William thinks. 'Babies.'

'*Babies?*' Lisa hoots.

'Well, yes, you know, there's quite a lot about them. When he first came to Italy and didn't like it very much, he noticed how they loved babies.'

'*Where Angels Fear to Tread* – it's so long since I read it,'
Fanny put in, 'but there's a baby in that, isn't there?'

'Yes. We were reading that this afternoon.'

'I know – they come from England to kidnap it, don't they?'
Fanny remembers. 'From Sawston. Or to buy it or something.
And there's a frightful accident – the carriage overturns and the
baby dies?'

'Not really an accident. Philip realises it wasn't fate but his
responsibility. I'm not sure about that myself.'

Lisa beams in triumph. 'Yes, I did read it! At school, I think.
Don't you remember, Jay? Did you ever read Forster? No one
does nowadays, do they. Except Willy.'

'Everyone's read Forster,' Jay says. 'It's simply that they've
forgotten.'

They have all seen the film before. With Buñuel's alarming
images, Jay and Lisa are at home, both enjoying themselves
more perhaps than they have done since they came to Italy.
Even William is happy enough. The thought of an exterminating
angel precludes fortuitous catastrophe and so lets one off the
hook, so to speak. He is not particularly interested in the
film-maker's attitude to the Catholic Church, nor is he able to
understand Spanish or to read more than sketchily the Italian
subtitles but he recognises the situation and would not be
astonished if, like the victims in the film, everyone seated in this
comfortable cinema were to find themselves imprisoned by an
invisible barrier. Would he behave better than most, he wonders,
since he has lived so long in expectation of the hail of bullets,
the flaming sword? He thinks he would feel as he did on the
plane – almost without fear once it was clear that his destiny
was out of his hands. Realising this, he grasps something else:
it is not extermination but the hope of evading it that terrifies
him. All he asks is to know what will happen next.

Fanny knows what will happen next and slips out from her seat
at the end of the row before the prisoners are freed, before the
service of thanksgiving when they will be trapped once again,
screaming in the church. That last burst of gunfire, somehow

she is not ready to hear it again. She may never be ready.

The dusk is calming. Nothing violent here. Fanny takes a deep breath and walks away from the cinema, up through the square past the albergo into the hedged and terraced gardens, following the scent of herbs crushed underfoot and the thin thread of Monteverdi in the night air, the one interwoven with the other; so the music is rosemary and thyme and suddenly very close, just on the other side of the hedge a sublime, declamatory statement as Fanny finds herself by a great bush of laurel at the parting of two ways: one down to the music, the other up a narrow path of irregular stone steps to a small garden she had not realised was there.

'You are not too cold?'

Fanny had thought herself alone but there, sitting in a stone niche on a marble seat is a little man whose feet barely touch the ground. Ivy curls from the wall behind his balding head, crowning him. Then he stands and the illusion of divinity, of Pan in the garden, is gone. He beams like a benevolent pixie.

'I am sorry, I made you jump. Felix Wanderman.'

'Fanny Farmer. I'm disturbing you?'

'Oh no. Not at all. But you are not at the music?'

'I'm running away from Buñuel.'

'Very wise. There is enough slaughter already, I think. Won't you sit down?' He offers the marble bench.

'I think I'd rather walk a bit. I had no idea this garden was here.'

'San Salvatore is full of surprises.'

'You've been here before?' Behind its high hedges this garden is less tended than the others. Fanny smells honeysuckle. She pulls a leaf as they walk in the blue darkness and rubs it between her fingers. Verbena.

'Yes, quite often. Ada has always liked it.'

'Your wife? Is she with you?'

'Always.' He speaks lightly, still smiling. 'She died a year ago. I loved her very much.'

'I'm so sorry.' How awkward are the English at receiving grief, Fanny thinks, and how simply he offers it, like a gift.

They have come to the edge where the hill falls away. Fanny

touches a balustrade. There is a crack where the stone has crumbled. An urn which spills flowers that in the night are grey, looks unsafe, it could be toppled, kill. She turns to say something to her companion and recognises him.

'Oh dear. I think we nearly met before, at Fiesole. You were in the white car.'

'You were in the coach?'

'No, we were in the Audi.'

'Ah.'

'It was awful. A terrible muddle. I do apologise. I hope you weren't hurt.'

'Not a scratch. I assure you.'

'I should really thank you for saving our lives.'

She cannot see his expression but he makes a gesture of dismissal.

'My own too. It was a reflex action. Interesting – the instinct to survive when one has no particular wish to live.' His tone is not self-pitying and no response seems to be asked for. 'You will be here for the Festa?'

'Festa?'

'The festival for the saint. At the end of September. A thanksgiving for one of the many times the Medicis were sent packing down the hill. This place has a violent history, as you will have gathered. A pity it has no future.'

'It seems to be doing well . . . Oh, you mean it's artificial. Yes, I've been feeling that. Too safe somehow? But I don't know it at all really. Perhaps, if you have time, you could tell me about it, show me around a bit?'

'It would be a pleasure. There are one or two corners not everyone gets to see. But you'll be off to Florence, no doubt.'

'Perhaps. I want to. But there's plenty of time. Thank you.'

Felix nods. Sad, he thinks, that to enjoy the company of women he must nowadays play the interesting little Jew with tales to tell. I was a man. Nevertheless he has taken to this young woman who does not care for Buñuel. Beneath her ease there is an air of nervy bravado, the kind he has seen in actresses waiting to go onstage.

Walking down from the garden to the laurel where they will

part, Fanny says: 'I wonder if it's even possible to find the real
Italy any more.'

'Ah. Yes. The real Italy,' says Felix gravely, then wishing her
a good night off he trots on his small feet, purblind under the
crescent moon. Moley going home.

At their side of the terrace (Michelangelo) Lisa and Jay are
entertaining the internationally known continental film director
with his harem, most of whom look old enough to appreciate
Jackanory. They must have met up in the cinema and are now
exchanging the names of acquaintances in the world of film which
girdles the globe from Hollywood and back again. They seem to
find it consoling, this naming of names. Stars, thinks Fanny,
closing Bronzino's shutters, and looking up sees a shower falling
from the sky. Streisand? someone says and another answers:
Beatty? Jean-Paul? Charlotte? Dirk?

Fanny salutes Vega and Orion and undresses and slips into
bed beside William. At some point she wakes or he wakes her
because she has called out.

'Sorry.'

'The dream? D'you want anything?'

'No. Well, yes, thank you.'

She drinks the Perrier. They kiss politely and lie down side
by side.

'I wonder if I shouldn't have got pregnant at all at my age?'

'It wasn't your fault. Fan, you must remember that. It was
an accident you got pregnant. It was no one's fault.'

'Yes. Of course.'

Fanny doesn't say: I wish we had buried him.

For a man who lives in such daily peril, William nips off to
oblivion (or whatever dangerous dreams he has) with amazing
ease.

Fanny, knowing that to seek sleep is to lose it altogether,
goes over in no particular order the events of the last few days.
She tells herself a story of the sightings and then the meeting
with Felix Wanderman, the plane, the flutter of nuns at Pisa,
the view of Santa Croce, the yellow helicopter, the stern bell
speaking at midday and the other answering, all the talk about

mushrooms, the muddle at Fiesole. Only at the last moment as the dark fur of sleep comes to cover her does the lost girl at the airport appear to Fanny – a wavering and tentative shade.

THREE

'The plane we came out on. That would be the flight back. It must be the same plane.'

Fanny has woken early and bought a copy of yesterday's *Herald Tribune* at reception. Not that she wants the news. She would prefer to be without it. Since arriving at San Salvatore it has been a positive pleasure not to know what is going on in the world outside (to pretend there is no world outside) but buying postcards she spotted the paper and so, of course, she bought it and passed it round at breakfast time.

'How awful,' says Lisa. 'It could have been us.'

Jay points out that by the laws of chance, the actual plane is irrelevant. The fact that their plane from Heathrow to Pisa was the one to be hijacked on its return flight made it no more likely that they might have been the victims than any of the millions in the air at the time all over the globe. He goes back to his yoghurt, grinning wickedly, knowing that he has enraged Lisa. (Since coming here there has been an ever so slight change in the nature of the relationship between these two; Lisa has stopped anticipating his every need, though she still makes sure he drinks his milk.)

Fanny says: 'I've always thought that sounded funny. You'd think the essence of chance would be that it had no laws.' She reads the report again, more closely. The Italian authorities are looking for the owner of a red Fiat with a dented offside bumper found parked in a no-parking area at Pisa airport. There is a connection here but she cannot quite place it yet.

'It's out of date. I wonder where they are now. It says here it might be Grey Wolf or Black Tuesday or an Armenian splinter group. I didn't know there was an Armenian group to splinter from.'

'It won't be Grey Wolf,' Lisa says. 'That's Italian right wing. Madly right. They don't hijack planes, they blow up railway stations. You remember – Bologna. Ages ago.'

'Oh yes.' Of course, it is Lisa's job to know about terrorists just in case Jay should ever be hijacked on one of his hundred flights a year. Fanny, looking out over the village and the walls and parapets, the terraces of olives, the cypress and oak, the hills like reflections of their own, the morning haze below that hides the plain, realises how she lives, how they all live, as if such fearful goings-on were news from elsewhere of someone else's hooligan children – a delinquency to be deplored but one that touches their own lives only if, like Jay, you are always on the wing; or planning a holiday in Israel; or splashing out on a trip to Cairo; or Christmas shopping in Knightsbridge or Oxford Street. Since no one the Farmers knew had time or inclination to shop in late December in either place even that horror had been a picture on television. Then and on the bloodstained occasions since, the nation has expressed its regret officially in full colour in that peculiarly English way that takes the sting from the pain and dulls the heart.

We are become lizards, Fanny thinks, watching a little gecko in frozen stillness on the wall. Our blood has thinned and runs cool. Did you know geckos can cry?

'We'd better not tell Willy,' she says.

'Why not?'

'Oh. You know Willy.' Fanny suddenly remembers and laughs. 'Do you know, there's a notice in reception: it says if you are leaving the Castello don't take your handbag. I asked whatsisname about it. Ferdi the Bull. And he said there are no pickpockets in Florence but they'll break your arm for your handbag.'

'Oh, Nando, you mean.' Lisa yawns and grins at once. 'He's teaching me Italian.'

So Nando is teaching Lisa Italian.

'Better not tell Willy what?' says Willy, stepping out on to the terrace. He has been lying in letting a number of pleasant considerations run through his mind. At first he had not been too keen on this trip (reports of cholera and typhoid feasting on trippers to the Mediterranean, rumours even of the Plague come again, a fear that this is exactly the kind of spot that attracts academics anxious to discuss structuralism, which he neither teaches nor understands). However, having agreed for Fanny's sake, William is quite pleased with the way things are going. He realises he is old-fashioned and under-motivated, possibly even sentimental, but chats about literature in a Tuscan garden seem infinitely attractive after the horrors of the Poly. He actually wishes to do some sight-seeing but meanwhile is happy enough to anticipate the glories of Florence and the possibilities of the villa at Fiesole. Above all, he feels safe here. He sees himself lying on the bed in the airy white room within the walls of the Castello and if he closes his eyes can return to a childhood cot with the murmur of benevolent voices outside and white curtains lifting their skirts in the breeze.

'What am I not supposed to know?'

'Oh nothing,' says Fanny, pouring his coffee. 'It's there in the paper. Just another hijack.'

Oh. Just another hijack.

William reads the report carefully, letting his coffee grow cold. He lights a cigarette.

'It was our plane.'

Getting closer, he thinks.

Fanny says: 'I'm writing postcards to Alison and Rob. What shall I say?'

Lisa yawns and stretches.

'What shall we do today?'

'No more Buñuel, thank you.'

'Florence?'

'We've missed the coach.'

'Coach?' says Jay, alarmed.

'It's the only way,' Fanny explains, trying not to laugh – he looks so startled, as well he might. As far as Jay is concerned coaches are things other people use, like camels. 'No one takes a car to Florence unless they're staying at a hotel with a guarded car-park. A coach leaves from the Castello every morning at ten. But we could get to Fiesole. We could take the car.'

At the idea of Fiesole William perks up again.
'I'll ask at reception about the Villa Inglese.'
'What villa?' says Lisa.

They plan to leave in an hour. In Bronzino Fanny sits alone at
the table by the window. She looks at the postcards. One shows
the Castello, the other a rather crude Madonna. Putting on her
spectacles and peering more closely, she sees what appear to
be dribbles of tomato ketchup on the cheeks of the Virgin. The
English caption reads: Santa Maria del Castello tears really for
the babies. Fourteenth century.

She thinks of writing the card, posting it, Alison or Rob picking
it up off the doormat and dropping it in the trash-can, or worse,
leaving it for her to find still on the hall floor on her return. She
looks again at the Madonna. Yes, one could weep tears of blood.
She puts the cards aside and opens her *Teach Yourself Italian*
marked with the page turned down from the last time she used
it, on their Argentario holiday. (Willy always winces at this habit
of Fanny's and he is right, of course.) The book is set out as a
continuing story, in the way of the children's Peter and Jane
books. (Fanny remembers that prim pair and the glee with which
she and the children parodied the little monsters, killing them
off with fates so horrible she can recall them now; also, how
Alison and Rob were then, Rob in particular doubled up with
small boy's laughter wanting her to tell it again and never to
stop. It is still Rob with whom she has a minimal communication.
That is to say he will sometimes sit, rolling his cigarette, knees
like knives tucked under his chin, and talk at her. But that is
something.)

It is Piero and Maria here, but they at least are adult although
their relationship is ambiguous. Fanny would skip to the end to
find out what happens but she is not advanced enough to
understand. Meanwhile they live (together?), so far as she can
make out, in a house with a red roof. They write each other
letters, so possibly they have quarrelled over the uncles, doors,
books, meals and animals that feature largely. So far Piero leads
rather a dull life, mostly in the garden (nel giardino), though
flicking ahead, Fanny sees that drama awaits. While Maria is

with the uncle in the study (nello studio) Piero falls from the tree and it is necessary to call Dr Rossi. A few pages on Maria is in the kitchen (nella cucina) with the baby (what baby?) and Piero at the dentist's asking for the police station (you'd think he'd know). Maria takes her baby (che bel bambino! Italians love babies) to the market and buys a mirror, sausages and a pin, unaware apparently that she is taking a train to Firenze with Piero, who is living out William's worst fantasies and some he has never thought of. A Rossini opera ensues as Piero – the chorus indifferent – cries out to a deaf world: Ho perduto il mio baule! My luggage is lost, the train departs, I have left my ticket at the inn; where is Giovanni? (who?) Where are my roses? Dov'è Maria? Dov'è il bambino? Dio mio! The train is departing! Maria has thrown the red roses out of the window of the train (del treno)! Addio! Addio!

Fanny is not writing postcards. Fanny is not teaching herself Italian. She is laughing her head off.

'I'm so sorry,' she says, opening the door, still laughing. 'Did you knock before?'

'Not at all.' Felix Wanderman has covered his pate with a linen sunhat with floppy brim of the kind children wore at the seaside fifty years ago. He seems shy. 'I thought perhaps, if you would still like to look round? When it's cooler but before it gets dark? But you will be busy.' In the daylight he looks even smaller.

'Yes, I'd love that. How kind of you. That would be lovely.'

'Well. If you still feel like it, I'm in Fra Angelico.'

Fra Angelico? Oh yes, of course.

'Yes, I know. *The Annunciation.*'

'That's right.' He looks brighter. What was the word? Chipper. That's it. Off he trots down the perilous steps, with one hand for the rail. 'Later then,' he waves.

'Later.' What a nice man.

What's got into Fanny?

'Oops,' she says as the car lurches on the bends. 'Vendo una vacca e compro un gatto. Now who in their right senses would sell a cow and buy a cat? I ask you?'

'What?'

'Something to do with EEC sanctions, I suppose. Milk mountains or whatever.'

'Fanny, what are you talking about?'

She has William's attention. He finally takes his nose out of the Blue Guide and looks at her.

'I'm learning Italian. If we have an accident I shall know exactly what to say, if I can remember it.' Speaking of accidents reminds her of Felix Wanderman and she opens her mouth to tell them, then decides to keep it to herself.

'Oh, good. Fine.' William is a little apprehensive, puzzled at least. He always thinks of Fanny as so open. There is something odd about her today, tingly. Has she really got over the stillbirth as well as it appears or is there a tension yet to be released? He takes her hand, squeezes it gently. Dimly he does understand what it is for a woman to carry a child and lose it. He who is never angry is angry at this moment with the children for not helping more, for being embarrassed. They turned away from it all. Rob said sorry once and kissed his mother on the cheek; Alison said nothing – she seemed, if anything, affronted, as if he and Fanny had been hatching some plot to trap her. She stayed away from home (where?) for a fortnight, coming back once or twice to steal from the fridge and the food cupboard (she even took a pheasant from the deep-freeze). Nowadays in the Farmers' circle you pretend you don't mind if your seventeen-year-old daughter disappears without explanation for a couple of weeks. But you do mind even while you know you mustn't ask. William is angry at this second but he has been worried lately about Alison. For the only time in his life he has wished it were possible still to be the autocratic father and lock up his daughter to keep her safe.

Now they are coming into Fiesole, Lisa negotiating the car sticking her head out of the open window to yell: Parking? William glances at Fanny, observing her delicate profile, fair skin that is freckled already and burns easily, the tilt of her head, her chin, the features narrow but strong. Round about forty these bones beneath were revealed, the true cartography of her spirit, and William had found her more beautiful than ever before. He thinks: she is brave. Also – she could break.

After the peace of San Salvatore, in Fiesole they are back in the world of action. Under a midday sun (not too hot at this time of year and at this altitude – more a gold that pours down over everything: vine leaves, walls, dust, the faces of young women) they are thirsty and settle outside the first café-bar to consult the Blue Guide, but are distracted by ordering drinks and the ceaseless motion of the Cathedral square. The bus arrives from Florence at the stop across the road and more seem to pour out than the small single-decker could possibly hold. Many, like those waiting to board, are carrying flowers. So the flowers go down the hill and flowers come up the hill, thinks Fanny; what are they for – saints' days? graves? A minibus that looks faintly familiar does not stop but takes the road up out of the square while a Vespa, driven rather wildly, deposits a girl and in a puff of dust, turns and is off again going down. Over the road and a little way up a busy market is in progress. The open-air bar under the vines that looks now more attractive than the road-side one they have settled for, was empty and in the blink of an eye is suddenly full as if by magic. People (Americans? Germans? English?) are occupying the tables, calling to each other, standing against the far wall to get the view. Down below, at the curve of the road, the big coaches doze on their high wheels behind tinted windows.

Lisa wants to go to the market. Jay is sweating in spite of the shade. He mops his brow with a large silk handkerchief. Fanny notices.

'I wish we could find somewhere really cool. What about the Cathedral?'

No – no one wants to go into the Cathedral.

'What does it say in the guide, Willy?'

'There's a Roman theatre. It must be just round the corner.'

'I'm famished,' says Lisa.

'But it's closed from twelve thirty till two o'clock. There won't be time before lunch.'

'Unless we take it with us.'

So they buy sandwiches in the café (they look almost like English sandwiches though the bread might be dry) and a bottle of wine and a bottle of mineral water and pile their lunch into Lisa's big sling bag.

The lavatory at the gatehouse is sensationally clean.

'Heaven!' says Lisa. Their glance meets in the small mirror. 'Are you all right, ducky?' Fanny is dragging a comb through her fine, crinkly hair. It always frizzes in dry heat. Sometimes (often) she envies Lisa's plait, the thick obedient hair you can do up in the morning and forget. She remembers gallumphing Lisa at some other time, caught in a moment of beauty against a window or it might have been in a garden, her legs planted wide, her strong neck bowed as she brushed her freed hair, the whole yard of it. It was a morning light.

'Fine.'

'Really?'

'Really fine. See you outside.'

It will soon be closing time in the theatre, which is not a theatre at all but an open place on the edge of a wide view; more like a garden with its olives and grass and terraces and warm stones.

As Fanny steps into the garden the bell sounds from the campanile and she cannot make out where everyone has gone. There seems to be a gardener or a guardian, a man in denims moving around with a hand-sickle between hedges and shrubs.

'Buon giorno,' she says and he answers. He says something she cannot understand, snaps off a leaf and offers it to her, showing with his fingers, she must rub. 'Inglese?' he says and she nods, smiling as she rubs and holds her fingers to her nose. Bay.

Stones that were seats – now she can see the shape of the amphitheatre – stones that were steps and walls, and here a large flat stone as big as a bed and an English mother calling to her children: it is time to leave the garden.

Fanny shields her eyes. There in the distance it must be Willy, reading his guide and looking up and in each direction to place everything, to name it. At the end of an avenue of stone Lisa is planted in the full sun, face flung back, she could be made of sun-worshipping stone, a full-breasted divinity, her long skirt clinging to her thighs and legs as a sculptor might have draped them.

Then in the deepest shade under a grouping of three olives a fat man rests, his head on a pillow of hummocky grass, a handkerchief over his eyes, and catching Jay unawares in this vulnerable posture Fanny thinks perhaps we are not after all set in our final moulds. She remembers how years ago sitting on a river bank under willows Jay told her that he had once been despairingly in love with an Englishwoman in Egypt. That was all he said. She had not loved him, or she had gone away. Fanny imagines his amorous ghost prowling the banks of the Nile while he sleeps here and suddenly wakes. Was he dreaming?

'Fanny.'

She takes his hand to help him up and at the same moment the statue of Lisa moves and William waves.

'Let's eat here.'

'It says no picnicking.'

'Everyone else has gone. They've closed.'

'Is that the gardener? Will he chuck us out?'

'We'll have to hide.'

They are whispering. They have recaptured the innocence of breaking small rules. They eat and drink and after the wine (even Jay has a swig) it is impossible not to fall asleep. The gardener finds them sleeping in the Roman temple. But there is to be no Italian opera after all, he does not disturb them and they do not wake until the gates are open again and other voices chase them from the garden.

They decide to go their separate ways. Lisa wants to treasure-hunt in the market and Jay is happy to wait for her in the better bar under the vines (empty now) where a cat yawns among the geraniums and measures the size and softness of his lap.

Fanny follows William and the Blue Guide up the long climb to the church of St Cecilia and the convent buildings of San Francesco (closed 12.00–15.00). It is exactly three o'clock as they arrive. While William goes into the church Fanny rests on a stone seat out of doors, a little dizzy from the wine. But the heat here is even more intense and on the steps of the church a seminar seems to be in progress in a language she does not understand. The students listen gravely and their leader speaks without pause like a talking machine, not loudly but relentlessly.

So Fanny is driven indoors, into the dark first rooms and passages. Dimly she makes out sorrowing tablets speaking in marble of disasters – floods, earthquake and deaths in China. She can hear voices that sound like whispers, secrets being exchanged (an acoustical freak), but sees no one, Willy is nowhere to be seen. Then suddenly she is out in a quiet place open to the sky, with dry flowers, a fresco of St Francis, brown-robed, barefoot, his hands open and raised in a cloud of birds; a real bird singing in a cage so that she wants to break the wire and free it but something in that place stills her. She breathes calmly. Cool, she thinks, peace, alone. Then at the end of the cloister a shadow unfolds, a girl with two wings of disconsolate brown hair, though she has changed her jeans for a patchwork skirt, unevenly hemmed and not too clean. She is sitting on the wall of the cloister with her feet up, her head bent over an amorphous piece of knitting.

'It's nice here, isn't it?'

'Yes, it's lovely.' Fanny feels that if she speaks too loudly or makes a sudden movement, the girl might turn into a brown sparrow and fly away. 'What are you knitting?'

Perry looks down at the grey bundle that might once have been white.

'Well, it was for Mario. But the shoulders don't look quite right, do they.'

'I'm afraid I don't know about knitting. You could always undo it and start again.' Now, Fanny says to herself, walk away this minute, don't get involved, find Willy, there is muddle here, don't stay, don't ask about the baby. 'Where's Mario?'

'Oh, he's in Florence with his granny. Well, it was a bit awkward but this boy said he'd give me a lift and I thought it would be all right just to come up here. It's so nice and cool. D'you think that was all right?'

'I expect if he's with his grandmother, he'll be fine.' Don't ask one more question. 'She's Italian?' (Italians love babies.)

'She's a cow.' Perry suddenly looks alarmingly as if she might cry. Fanny wishes William would find her and everything would be ordinary again. 'I know I shouldn't say that. But when I got there Sergio had gone, you see, and I don't speak Italian. Sergio had said they'd look after him. I'm sorry, I didn't mean to go on like this. I feel much better up here – it's so lovely and quiet. Florence is horrible.'

Fanny feels herself on the edge of a world where accidents really happen, luggage is lost, and it is not only in operas and Italian lessons that the train departs, roses are thrown from the window, and babies mislaid. Dov 'è il bambino? She should never have asked. She always does – rush in with the fools while angels disapprove. Now, at the moment she might murmur something, smile and go and look for Willy, she knows even before she speaks what she will say.

'There's a camp-site where we are. Up at San Salvatore. I don't know but I shouldn't think it's expensive. There's nothing much to do – '

'Oh, that sounds lovely if it was just Mario and me. But while I've been up here I've been thinking, and I know Sergio will come back. Then everything will be all right. I'd got in a muddle down there.'

'Well then. If you change your mind. By the way, my name's Fanny Farmer and my husband is William.'

'I'm Perry.'

'Yes, I remember. Is that short for something?'

'Perdita. Something out of Shakespeare, I think. Silly, isn't it?'

'I think it's rather pretty.' Fanny glances at the girl with the name out of Shakespeare. She is watching the yellow bird as it hops around its cage. How do you tell nowadays about the young? They have unclassed themselves. The signals have changed. Is she really a waif or is that just another of the postures?

They sit quietly. The girl has returned to her shyness or her silence or her natural passivity. She looks to Fanny about twelve, yet she has borne a baby and brought herself to Italy, and is in some kind of trouble.

There is the sound of approaching voices: the earnest students from the steps.

'Well, I must go and find my husband.'

'Thank you ever so much.'

Fanny shakes her head.

'I wish they'd let that bird out of its cage.'

Willy is disappointed because the Blue Guide says there is a Chinese collection and he cannot find it.

They walk down some steps and across to the further wall where a flock of sharp-calling female American tourists are photographing each other against a view that will never come out, so they will have to explain what the view would have been and will enjoy explaining. There is something about them, a resemblance, as though they all belonged to the same family of tanned fearless sisters with strong features and clear eyes, zipping round Europe on American Express. The men, Fanny wonders, what do they do with their men?

What is Willy talking about?

'Oh, I suppose it was washed away in a flood. They've had a lot.'

'Flood?' Startled, Willy looks around as though expecting to be immediately engulfed. 'Up here? But it's so high.'

'If that's what flumen means.'

'Yes. Well, river really. A stream of anything – water, blood, tears.'

Fanny remembers something. Santa Maria del Castello really tearing for the babies. Blood. Or tomato ketchup.

'D'you remember the girl on the plane? Perry? With the baby?'

'Who? Oh, yes.'

'I just bumped into her in the cloisters.'

Willy nods. 'I say, look, there's the Brunelleschi dome. It's an incredible view.' Florence below is in a mist, the Cathedral and Cupola suspended, rootless shapes. He puts his arm round Fanny's waist. 'Florence. We really must go.'

Fanny peers down into the mist. There is the Renaissance. Where is the baby?

Yes, oh yes. We must go to Florence.

As Fanny and William walk down the hill through the park there is a chatter in the ilex wood and among the dark trees on the winding paths wimples bob in gossip: the nuns from the minibus out on a spree.

Jay has snoozed away the afternoon under the vines. If he drank he might have been Bacchus recumbent. A vine-leaf has fallen on his ample lap which the cat leaves reluctantly. Now the heat has gone out of the sun there is a snap of geranium in the air. Lisa has worn herself out in the market and found nothing, but requiring booty of some kind has come back with a fairly hideous plaster Madonna.

'Isn't it awful! Too frightful to resist. D'you think it might be lucky?' Anyway, she drops the dreadful doll in her big bag and recovers her spirits. 'It might look better later.'

They are all tired. Lisa drives.

'Just a sec,' Willy says. 'Can we go down that way first?'

'Willy! That's where we nearly had the accident.'

The iron gates, the screening trees, the hint within of a sharper fresher green, water perhaps.

Fanny opens her eyes. 'That's the Villa Inglese,' William says.

'D'you want to stop? I don't think we can here anyway.'

'No. Ferdinando says he can get us in. Another day.' The truth is, now he is here William is not at all sure if he wants to go in or not. Looking for Mr Forster.

Even though they have missed the Cathedral, the museum, the church of Santa Maria Primerana, the Etruscan remains and the view of Montecéceri, Fiesole has exhausted them. They return to the Castello hardly speaking. A scrap is in the air. There might be thunder. Jay's stomach is troubling him, which seems to irritate Lisa. She drives badly, jerking into gear, taking blind precipitous corners too fast. Damn, she says. Blast. Knickers. No one laughs. Fanny is reminded of the children going home in the car after a picnic, nervily awake and fractious. She has a headache. She closes her eyes again and opens them only when they are safely back within the Castello. They avoid the restaurant and agree to eat separately in their own quarters. Duck, says William as he sees Miss Head and Miss Stimpson coming towards them. I thought you liked them? Lisa is cross because Jay won't come to Buñuel. (Jay is in considerable pain though he would never say so. Lisa knows he is in pain.) His stupid stomach, she says and actually stamps her foot. There are stains of sweat between her breasts and under her armpits, spreading. The sky is clear but the air is punishing them. Fanny is now wide awake, possessed by her headache. Something is wrong with the shower. I've got the curse she says but William is asleep already. She doesn't want to sleep but at once she is in the dark pit of a dream. She does not hear when Felix Wanderman comes to the door of Bronzino, taps lightly, pauses and goes away.

High above the heads of the sleepers the plane that was hijacked at Pisa is still in flight while as Fanny turns mumbling in her dream the military jet crashes into the Apennines. It may have been sabotaged or suffered engine failure. Unless, of course, it was struck by lightning. In any case the wreckage settles and lies there quietly in the white and silent snow.

FOUR

Domani.

We will go to Florence/Rome/Venice tomorrow says Fanny's
book. Rome/Florence/Venice is the most beautiful city in Italy.
Domani, she says to herself (with emphasis on the second
syllable), with eyes closed not to cheat but finger in the page.
Oggi.

'Oggi' she says to William.

'What?' William is reading again. William is always reading.
He is vaguely aware that at some point in his life he cannot place
he gave up talking for reading. Not teaching: teaching is not
talking but telling. He may even have given up life for books.
That idea shocks him. He considers it while he waits politely for
Fanny to repeat her remark. Everyone is dozy today. The storm
sat for a while over San Salvatore but did not break. While Fanny
dreamed all night William woke in the early hours, regretting
his evening nap, and tried to concentrate on the issue of moral
responsibility in the works of E. M. Forster. But this was too
wide a question for such an hour of the night and in any case
too didactic for his present mood. It was just as well he did not
have to teach Forster. His attitude was at the best subjective,
at the worst woolly: fine for tea in the garden with Winifred
Stimpson and Cecily Head but unthinkable for the Poly.

What he found really interesting, now he came to think about
it, lying as still as he could in the darkness, was why, for
instance, Philip Herriton did not marry Caroline Abbott when
they seemed so perfectly suited. Well, she refused him, of
course, because she believed herself in love with Gino. She *was*
in love with Gino, Forster made that quite plain and one had to
accept it, just as Philip had done. What was it she said? 'Body

and soul' – that was it. She was body and soul in love with Gino and yet in a way the true romantics were Gino and Philip, who worshipped her. Maybe men always were the romantics in love.

He was wider awake than ever, reached for the book beside his bed, half-remembering something, but he could not turn on the single light without waking Fanny and his torch was in the toilet-bag in the bathroom.

William let his thoughts wander, to catch sleep unawares. The trip today, the amphitheatre and the forbidden picnic in the garden. We were happy then, all of us. Weren't we?

At the last moment before his eyes closed the phrase he could not look up came back to him: 'For all the wonderful things had happened.' He smiled and slipped into a dreamless sleep.

'Today,' Fanny repeats. 'Oggi. Oggi we will not go to Florence I suppose.'

'I suppose not.' He reaches for the coffee. Is she all right this morning? Her skin looks tightly drawn, a little pinched. Worship – is that what he feels? Does he worship her? Years ago, before they were married, when they were parted William would beg or steal something of hers to keep by him, a handkerchief, a favour. He had the feeling at the time that she didn't approve. Perhaps she was simply surprised that he should need such tokens. Since then there have been the years between them, the children, the fibre and flesh of marriage, such questions have not come up; although he still is not sure what she really felt about the child they lost, how much she suffered and may be suffering now.

'Well, it's a funny word, isn't it? Oggi?'

'Yes, it is.'

Fanny says: 'What's happened about your Villa Inglese?'

'I went to reception before breakfast. Ferdinando said he'd get us in.'

'I know. When did he say? Today?'

'Oh, you know Italy. Tomorrow, he says. Always tomorrow.' Fanny laughs.

'Domani.' She looks up at the sky. 'Italy. Remember Venice?'

(She means do you remember us in Venice? Before the children. Before the years piled up.) She wrinkles her brow. 'Everything had to be right then, didn't it? It doesn't matter so much now. Thank God.'

'What?'

'Perhaps that's growing up? Accepting muddle. D'you think it'll rain? It's still heavy.'

William knows what she means about age, time, marriage. But for him still Muddle holds the seeds of Chaos. If the white car had not swerved at the bend at Fiesole. If at Pisa they had been departing not arriving.

'I've thought of something,' Fanny says. 'It's just come to me.'

'Mmm. And what's that?'

'The paper yesterday – the red Fiat with the dented bumper they found at the airport. We passed it on the road to Florence. It was going the other way to Pisa.'

'There are a lot of red Fiats in Italy.'

'Yes, of course.' Fanny remembers about Willy. 'And it probably had nothing to do with it anyway. The hijack, I mean. I expect people leave red Fiats at Pisa airport every day.' All the same, she thinks, connections. They please her (even this one) ever since childhood: fairy-tales – paths crossing, journeys ending where they began; an invisible web spread over the globe, through time and space. Perdita lost and found.

'Oh dear. I still haven't written to the children.'

'Write domani.'

'Yes. Tomorrow. Unless we go to Florence?' Fanny has finished her breakfast. She wishes she still smoked. She wonders what to do. Paint? Learn Italian? Learn to do nothing? We have forgotten how. 'What's yesterday?'

William thinks. French helps. So does Latin. 'Ieri?'

'I think we did too much yesterday.'

Today, oggi, Jay will stay in bed. Lisa, who has a gift for sleep, has got over yesterday's temper (last night they screened *The Discreet Charm of the Bourgeoisie* and *The Pink Panther*). In the airy upstairs room of Michelangelo she has plumped up Jay's pillows while he showered, put him back into bed, tucked him up under the cool white sheet, unplugged the telephone (an extra which is not normally optional at San Salvatore but even on holiday Jay, of course, must be instantly available to any of his connections all over the world in case a deal comes up in Hollywood or collapses in Hong Kong). She has given him his breakfast, his stomach medicine and his pills, set out his side table with the same stomach medicine and pills together with Perrier and a couple of biscuits that look remarkably like Farex, pulled down the blind halfway against the sun and on second thoughts plugged in the telephone after all, just in case he should be taken ill or make his stomach worse worrying about being out of touch.

'There!' says Lisa, and Fanny, come to visit, cannot help a smile. Jay sitting up in bed looks so young, stripped of the years (though his multitudinous worldly concerns are doubtless still whizzing round inside his head). He wears clean white silk pyjamas and raises his face obediently as Lisa bends to peck his cheek. 'Well, if you'll really be all right.'

'I'll be fine.'

Fanny observes that there is only one toothbrush in the rack above the handbasin. So Willy was right.

'What are you going to do, Lisa?'

'Oh, bake myself black in the sun. I might have an Italian lesson. Don't worry, ducky. I'll pop back.'

'No need,' says Jay.

'An Italian lesson?' says Fanny.

Lisa laughs. She has strong, very white teeth. Sometimes she reminds Fanny of Hotlips in M.A.S.H.

'Well, it's time I learned something, isn't it? You're all so clever and I'm pig-ignorant.'

'Poor Jay,' says Fanny when Lisa has gone, her toy-bag packed for a week on the Riviera. One of the pleasures of friendship with Jay is silence. Fanny stands at the foot of the bed, looking at him. It strikes her suddenly (a William thought) that they have all lived with Jay's stomach so long it has become like a dog around the house. Yet it could kill him. Jay could die. She could not bear a Jayless world and wonders why, since she came to Tuscany, she has had thoughts of death in the very home of life. Of course she could bear it. One does. But it would be a gentleness lost, a peace. 'I've brought you *Paris Match*. And Gombrich if you're up to it. D'you want anything else?' Jay shakes his head.

'I expect I'll sleep.'

'Does it hurt?'

'I ride it. I've got the knack by now. Lisa fusses. Bless you – off you go. Where's Willy?'

'Up to something with his girl-friends, I think. Stead and Simpson.'

'Oh yes.'

'I could stay.'

'Better not to talk too much. I'll be fine tomorrow.'

'Of course you will. Domani then.'

'Domani. Ciao.'

'Domani. Sleep tight.'

As Fanny closes the door quietly behind her she hears the telephone, that funny foreign ring, Jay's connections.

When she gets back to Bronzino William has gone but there is a note under the door. Fanny is puzzled. Who would be writing to her? She reads it once, squinting, then puts on her spectacles and takes it to the window. She reads it again, lets it fall to her lap and looks out on San Salvatore where there is still movement as always, but less than usual. Perhaps it is the weather. Or everyone did too much yesterday? They have slept late, it is already noon.

Willy has left his binoculars on the window-seat and Fanny takes off her spectacles and picks them up. There in one of the upper gardens is Lisa sunbathing, flat on her back, arms spread, head tipped back, topless. That is probably all right in San Salvatore. Anything you fancy seems to be all right here. There is the continental film director with his nymphets. They have occupied the children's playground and the girls swarm over the climbing frames and slides and ride the swings very high. In the shade of the big chestnut a small child watches. Why are the grown-ups playing?

Fanny peers further out beyond the walls where campers, who must also have slept late, are moving around, stretching, washing, cooking, greeting, making patterns of which they are unaware, that can only be spied from a distance. And there, beyond all, is the tower. Does the tower watch? The yellow helicopter is landing now on the patch of earth by the tower.

This is sanctuary, thinks Fanny, a safe place. No muddles here. No Italy either. Where are the people? Ieri, yesterday, Maria and Piero and the gardener and the uncle and the animals (though probably not the doctor or the dentist or the chemist) lived here – really lived – inhabited these houses, hung their washing across the narrow streets (guests of the Castello are prayed to use the automatic laundry behind the hall of reception), shouted from window to street to window: where is the uncle, where is the grandmother, where is the baby? (They wouldn't let me see him, they took him away, I knew before they did when the foetal heart had stopped. He should have been named, buried; it is dangerous to evade rituals.) Where are the red roses? Maria threw them from the window and lives now in a high-rise flat in Milan. Maria works in a shop. Piero works in a factory. The flat is too small. Maria, Piero, the uncle and the grandmother live in the small flat. Where is the garden? Where are the animals? Today Maria throws the baby from the window.

The weather and the curse have made Fanny heavy. She decides not to learn Italian today, not to paint. She looks again at the note in her lap. Fra Angelico it says. She studies the plan and compares it with the real, three-dimensional San Salvatore. She finds her sunhat and shoulder-bag and slips on her most comfortable sandals. Just as she puts out her hand to the door it is opened from the other side and a middle-aged woman carrying bucket, mop and dusters, her hair tied back in a red kerchief, is standing on the step.

'Buon giorno,' she says. 'Excuse.'

'Oh yes, of course. Please come in.'

How silly of me, Fanny thinks. The place is always clean – someone must clean it. She stands aside.

'Grazie, signora.'

'No. Thank you. Grazie.' The woman is politely brisk, doesn't care if Fanny stays or goes, but Fanny feels some exchange is called for. She feels the responsibility of courtesy. A tip when they leave, of course, but meanwhile what? Does she speak English? Can Fanny speak Italian? 'E caldo oggi.'

The woman speaks back, smiling, she is pleased that the foreigner has attempted Italian. What is the woman saying? Fanny smiles and nods. The woman smiles. Fanny makes a gesture with her hand: I am leaving, goodbye.

'Addio.'

Apparently that is funny. It must have been wrong.

'Arrivederci. A domani, signora.'

'Farmer,' says Fanny. 'Signora Farmer.'

More smiles.

'Mi chiamo Maria.'

Fanny jumps.

The 12.30 coaches have arrived. The Japanese are getting taller, one hears, but they still seem quite small, small as children next to the same sharp jawed American giantesses who had been photographing each other yesterday at San Francesco. Each party follows its own guide up and down and round San Salvatore, crossing each other's paths, meeting sometimes at the same corner but never quite colliding (if they were to collide the Japanese would be trampled to death). There is no danger that either will invade the small, high-hedged garden where Lisa, still bra-less, is baking her back before she goes for her Italian lesson at two o'clock. The Japanese cannot see over the hedge and the American matrons will cluck with shock and gallop on.

Jay is quite safe in bed discussing on the telephone invisible money with Sydney, Australia, where it is 9.30 p.m. and signs of spring are stirring while the leaves of Tuscany crackle gold on the vine.

Willy too is oblivious of the invasion, walking more heartily than he is accustomed with Misses Stimpson and Head who have promised him a view and are determined that he shall have

it. Miss Head leads, Miss Stimpson, though she has longer legs
suffers from thinner feet and falls behind, fluttering (flirting?) at
William who is concentrating on breathing and wishing he had
worn socks. Since we were young, she breathes (she is still
young, William thinks, a girl in disguise) – she snags her long
skirt on a twig, they brush against a dry tree, wade through
crisp leaves, breathe air of pure conifer. Since we were young
and found the view, blue violets everywhere, you would never
believe. Like Lucy Honeychurch? Oh yes, but in spring, of
course, no violets now. Then a deeper breath, a duck of the
head beneath the wavy brim of the sunhat and a smile, quite
naughty: the buoni uomini, you remember, the good men, Lucy's
muddle with the driver that led to everything – today we have
a buon uomo, a good man. Yes, she is flirting and William is
moved. A good muddle? he says, reaching to help her as she
stumbles and regains her balance and looks up into his face still
holding his hand quite firmly: Oh yes! A splendid muddle! At
that moment a voice summons them from above, only a few
yards away although Miss Head cannot be seen for the winding
route and leaves. But she has her view, she has arrived, she
calls them again with the certain, triumphant ring of one who
has navigated all hazards to reach the summit: 'Ecco!'

Miss Stimpson and William sink to the ground at their leader's
feet. Miss Stimpson is watching William anxiously. It was
worth it? She wants to give him this gift of the view. That
will be enough for her today – more than enough – and for
many days; in winter in Finchley Park she will look through
her Italian sketch-book (only pastel, I'm afraid, but sometimes Cissie says, not bad) and remember his face, bony, a little
sad or shy perhaps, but now he is smiling. Oh yes, he likes the
view.

'You can see Florence on a good day but there is the Castello
– doesn't it look a long way down – and Fiesole. And look – no,
that way – that hill there, not quite as high as ours, the one with
the chapel on top, right outside the Castello walls, you can't
even see it from down below, can you, Cissie? There was a
Roman temple there and the Etruscans before that. It's interesting, isn't it, Cissie, but not as open as this. Oh, look – isn't that

someone starting up the path to the chapel? Just there, above the Castello?'

Oh dear, Cissie always says I talk too little or too much.

Miss Stimpson takes off her floppy hat to fan her face.

William is resting, leaning to one side on his right elbow, enjoying the view but even more enjoying Miss Stimpson enjoying the view. Somehow the undefeated girl in this woman of what? – sixty? sixty-five? – is not ridiculous. He would have liked not to be English at that moment, to be able to take her hand and kiss it but all he can do is to say: 'Oh, yes, it's a lovely view.'

(The truth about William is that he is not much of a man for views. He is not insensitive. He can see what people mean and was impressed by the vista yesterday from San Francesco but not moved. This is a point where Fanny and he diverge. She will run to the edge for the view but he prefers the particular – the domestic outlook, the quince outside his study window, the objet trouvé, the arrowhead on the Downs, the George IV coin he dug up in the vegetable patch. In the famous Corot of Florence it is the black-robed figure in the foreground he wonders about. Now at this moment he is watching a sturdy ant carrying what appears to be a small twig across his immediate line of vision. The ant disappears and William lies back, eyes closed, and eases his sore feet in his espadrilles.)

Miss Head has laid out a picnic. She must have been carrying it in the small back-pack.

'Win and I go a long way on high-fibre biscuits but I popped in a sandwich for you. I daresay men prefer sandwiches.'

'You're spoiling me.'

'My father always took sandwiches on a hike. He could have had egg and cress but he preferred corned beef.'

'D'you always go on holiday together?'

'Of course.' Miss Head seemed surprised at his question. 'We rub along, don't we, Win?'

'Oh yes.'

'Forty years, is it?'

'It must be forty years.' Miss Stimpson looks vaguely surprised.

'Always Italy?'

Miss Head has snapped her large brown biscuit in half. She chews neatly and fiercely.

'We've strayed from the path. Greece. The Atlas mountains. But we always come back. Win gets seasick, you know.'

'Isn't it spoiled for you now? Trippers and so on?'

Miss Head produces a boy-scout knife and contemplates a nectarine.

'There's still the real Italy, if you know where to look. Isn't there, Win?'

But Win does not hear her. She has finished her high-fibre lunch and is standing, sunhat in hand, at the very edge of the famous view. She has taken off her sandals. She looks as if she might take wing, leap out and soar over cypress and birch and olive, over the Castello and Fiesole and Florence itself.

As William joins her she says: 'I could die here, I think.'

'It is wonderful. I am grateful.'

'Are you? I'm so glad.' She turns and looks directly at him, as though trying to fix something. 'I wish there had been violets,' she says, and then is flustered again.

At two o'clock, the siesta hour, they have gone to sleep in Sydney, Australia, and not yet woken in Hollywood, so Jay can nap. His breath comes in puffs, his stomach rises and falls steadily in gratitude for this quietus. He dreams that he is asleep.

Lisa, full of sun, rises, puts on her thin muslin top but not her bra, and makes her way out of the garden. Her direction is apparently aimless but she knows where she is going and what time it is. If anyone asked she would say she was going for her Italian lesson but no one will for San Salvatore is in a daze of sleep. Even the Japanese students of Dante, who do not sweat, are squatting in a neat circle under the trees at the picnic-site while their leader reads (in Japanese): In the middle of my life I found myself in a dark wood. Even the American women have put aside their cameras and hardly speak at all.

*   *   *

And while Miss Stimpson is speaking of violets the two figures she had spotted leaving the Castello have passed from the olive grove to the deeper dusk of ilex. This wood, that seems to Fanny almost impenetrable (though Felix knows his way and scampers up with remarkable speed) is the coolest spot of all on the whole of Monte San Salvatore.

'Would this be *The Annunciation*?' Fanny said, having made her way after several wrong turnings, to Fra Angelico which turned out to be in the less chic quarter of the Castello. Pin-clean again but no sun, which today was a relief. Though there was a distinct whiff of rotting rubbish. She had wondered what they did with it.

'Thank you for your note. I'm not disturbing you?'

'Indeed no. Please come in.' Felix had been at his desk, hardly hoping for Fanny, but here she was. He made a gesture with his hand that dismissed, would have swept away, his heap of books. 'Our little excursion then? I'm so glad you could come.'

The small man looked more in proportion in the cell-like room – apart from the books very tidy, Fanny noticed. There seemed nowhere to sit but Felix was already reaching for his linen hat.

'You're working. Are you sure I'm not interrupting?'

'I was working,' he corrected her, planting his hat firmly on his head. He beamed. 'Now I am on holiday. Come!'

'You have seen the so-famous *Annunciation*?'

'Only in books. I'm afraid we haven't looked at any pictures yet. Just a bad fresco of St Francis. But we'll be going to Florence, of course.'

'Ah yes. Of course one must go to Florence.'

They are leaving the grounds of the Castello by a path that leads past the tower and into the trees. As it enters the wood it narrows. The cool is welcome. Fanny breathes more easily, the scent of conifer is like ozone and the many shades of green refreshing. The eye needs green, she thinks. That staring blue is too much.

'You write then?'

Again that dismissive gesture.

'Dry-as-dust history no one reads.' Having climbed quickly so far, they pause for a moment in a spot where the wood is less dense and they are standing in filtered sun on a natural platform. Felix takes off his hat and mops his brow. His pate, Fanny observes, still looks a painful pink between flecks of calamine. 'Though I must admit,' he confides, 'I am rather enjoying Proverbs.'

'Proverbs?'

'About the woman of worth. "Her children arise up, and call her blessed; her husband also, and he praiseth her. Many daughters have done virtuously, but thou excellest them all."'

'Yes, that's beautiful.'

'And Jewish. You know, the Jews are much happier than we are given credit for. We are not always seated on a low stool sprinkling our heads with ashes and singing Lamentations. Though that is beautiful too.'

'You're researching?'

'Yes. Both Testaments. I enjoy that most of all – the research. Shall I confess something wicked? I am looking forward enormously to Christianity!'

Fanny laughs. She likes Felix Wanderman.

'Where is your husband today?'

'Walking, I think. Perhaps we'll meet him.' The heart of her husband trusteth in her. Yes, she hopes (believes) it does. Her children however do not call or not as the prophet meant. Except for the lost one. She smiles to herself. Would a Jewish Willy find comfort in Lamentations or Job – his afflictions formalised? As it is, he suffers but has been brought up as an upright Englishman, not to complain. They are climbing again. The wood grows denser. Unseen birds call. There is a heavy, winged displacement of oak leaves and an amber-eyed owl takes off awkwardly directly across their path. 'Oh dear, we woke him up.' The owl was a little too close for Fanny's comfort, it had the strangeness and suddenness of a portent. Nonsense. What is there to fear here? Every so often a window the size of a porthole yields a glimpse of the surrounding country. Up there – are those figures or statues on the edge of the promontory? 'I was thinking about the people, where they went. And the

Marchese. That must be his helicopter? You've been here before. D'you know him?'

'Just once we met him. Ada liked to meet people. You could say he has saved San Salvatore. He has also destroyed it. I have heard he is political, though who is not in Italy? But he is on the violent edge.'

'Does he keep a mad wife in that tower?'

'At least three, I am sure.'

For a while they do not speak. The track is now narrower than ever and precipitous, air and light gone. Felix remembers his banished pills and wonders if he is an old fool. If he were to leap into the darkness here. That would not be so bad – a kind of bomba. But unfair to his companion who does not even know where they are going. Ah, there are the steps – not far now.

Fanny too notices the flags of stone set in the path, so well-trod they seem part of the earth itself, and then a handrail and the steps widen, the forest retreats, the trees and shrubs appear ordered, intended. A scrap of blue, a handkerchief and the sky is open to them. At the moment she emerges from the tunnel of the wood she sees Felix panting and beaming on a seat, a hedge that might contain a garden, a building like a church or chapel beyond and a tablet, beautifully cut in marble in the way of Italian public notices: SANTA MARIA DEL CASTELLO: IL CIMITERO DEI BAMBINI.

'You're thirsty?'

'Oh yes.'

'There is water.'

'Up here? So high? It's cool. Lovely. But what does that mean? Cemetery?'

The blue has drained from the sky. It is white. Felix thinks he will stay where he is, just catch his breath, you know, one forgets what a climb. Ada used to run up. At least they should be safe from a guide here – no road. Yes, of course, Fanny must look round – it's quite a curiosity. In a little while Felix will explain.

'You'll be all right?'

*   *   *

Fanny knows, she has known certainly since she saw the notice, possibly all the way up, that this is not a garden but a graveyard and the toppling ancient stones mark graves so small only children could lie here. There are a few bunches of withered flowers but none of the paraphernalia – plastic bouquets, photographs of the deceased, towering angels – that distinguish most Italian cemeteries. Instead weeds, an immense laurel, a rose gone wild.

It is peaceful and shaded but even so her eyes take a moment to adjust to the deeper shadows of the chapel. No lock, no guide, she has it to herself except for a dry sound in the very margins of darkness where slender pillars support the low vaulted ceiling: bats or mice? In this quiet unguarded place, with peeling frescoes that remind her of children's drawings, Fanny senses a presence so powerful she would have fallen to her knees had she not at that second of surprised reverence recognised the figure to the side of the simple altar: Santa Maria del Castello tearing for the babies, ketchup and all.

Undusted and unwashed, this grubby-faced Madonna is less garish than the Lady of the Postcard, her blue gown grey, her plaster face dipped to the clumsy doll-like Christ child who reaches with one fat, stiff arm as if to grasp the Mother's breast. She is wonderful and awful, thinks Fanny and, looking round first, puts out her hand to touch the orange-red drops on that dusty cheek, when the door slams behind her.

Not the guardian of the place, not God, not Pan risen from the grove, but Felix feeling better. For five minutes on the seat outside he had really worried as his heart crashed its complaint.

'I'm sorry. I made you jump. I see you've found her.'

'Isn't it extraordinary? Look,' says Fanny and stoops to the Virgin's cobwebbed hem where plastic flowers, white and blue, are scattered, and tiny rolled-up messages like letters from a mouse. A couple are relatively fresh. Most are faded. 'Per Lucia sempre secura,' she reads, 'Antonio in pacem in aeternam. What is it? What does it all mean? The blood? The children?'

'The Plague,' Felix says. 'Or one of them. Perhaps it was cholera. The Plague came to Florence in 1438 – there may have been a connection. All we know is that the Castello largely survived. It was the children who died and by public order were buried here, away from the village. The chapel was built – it was a site of early worship, probably pre-Roman. Later the Madonna was installed – rather crude, you can see, possibly the work of a village carpenter with nineteenth-century sentimental improvements – and was said to weep blood at the time that is now the Festa. Over the years two occasions of thanksgiving became confused, a military victory over the marauding Medici and the remembrance of the children.'

'But some of these notes look almost fresh? And yet the place is so neglected.'

'Superstition? Myth? A few climb the hill hoping for intercession. Those who have lost infants. It depends if you believe.'

'In what?'

'Miracles.'

'This font. Are children still christened here?'

'Not in living memory. As you will have observed there are few babies born now in San Salvatore.'

Fanny feels quite calm and at the same time totally insane. Little Felix has seen more than she realises from behind his pebble glasses. The wisdom of Jews, he is sick of it, eternally sick, yet he does see sometimes. He would rather not. He pretends to a cheerfulness he does not feel.

'But there is another surprise. If you can climb a few yards further?'

The white sky has thickened while they have been in the chapel. The awaited storm might break. Fanny looks out over the tiny graves and wishes she were not English, she could wail and prostrate herself at the feet of the vulgar Madonna, add her own note to the other telegrams of grief and trust: if he is with you, keep him, love him, in aeternam, the one without name or grave. Instead though, she follows Felix a few more yards. He is nimbler now, she heavy with curse.

'There!' he says and she looks to see what he is talking about, what is so remarkable among the heaped stones at the top of the hill where all hope of nature's obedience to man is given up

and there is nothing beyond this clearing but stunted forest and
then hill after parched hill.

'A spring! So high up?'

'Quite pure. You can drink.' He cups his hands and water runs
down his face, his head, his spectacles, so that he has to take
them off and wipe them. And while Felix is purblind Fanny does
drink, and only in drinking realises how thirsty she was. Then
she is weeping, tears and water mingled; at last she can cry and
the first warm drops of rain fall on their heads.

'Water,' she says, 'so much water!'

'And more to come. We'd better go.'

'I lost a child, you see,' Fanny says and Felix nods, although
he can hardly have heard for the first thunderclap. She smiles.
The day, the water, the crude Virgin, Felix's company, everything, something has made her smile.

There is the cemetery again and the handrail and flight of now
slippery steps. The sky has cracked, they must hurry, it will be
more dangerous going down than coming up. But Fanny looks
back, her eyes drenched, for one last glimpse of the garden of
small graves.

Dove sono i bambini?

Here. Here they are.

The thunder wakes Jay at the same moment the telephone rings
(5 p.m. in Italy, approximately six hours later in Hong Kong)
but the storm cuts the line at the moment of connection. The
connection between Lisa and Nando of reception is also broken;
it is time for Nando to go back to work and Lisa to groan, shower,
and run home through the punishing rain to Michelangelo and
Jay, who might be worried or lonely.

William and Miss Head and Miss Stimpson got back just in
time to miss the storm. When Fanny comes in, soaked, William
is sitting up on the bed reading Luciano Berti's *Florence and its
Art* with preface by Sir Harold Acton. Fanny looks rather wild
and wet but he is thankful to see her and fusses around with
towels and tea.

'You weren't really worried?'

He kisses her, he puts her under a warm shower, he dries

her face, wraps her in a blanket, folds his arms around her like wings. He would like to make love to her now, without words or fears or stories.

'I thought you'd been struck by lightning.'

FIVE

Domani has become oggi. Today we are going to Florence.

All night it rained but the morning in San Salvatore is fresher, the sky clear. Such weather, everyone says, is unusual for September. It is in October they hope for rain to swell the olives. 'What a night!' Miss Head calls up to the window of Bronzino and Fanny waves back.

Everyone, even those who are not going to Florence, is afoot early this morning. 'Are we going to Florence?' Lisa says. She walks down to reception to tell Nando there will be no two o'clock Italian lesson and, coming out, meets William. 'Cancelling my Italian lesson,' Lisa says. In reception William asks again about the Villa Inglese. Felix Wanderman is looking for yesterday's *Herald Tribune* but it has not yet arrived. He picks up *La Nazione* from the reception desk. Military jet crashes in Apennines. He can read Italian headlines. Hijacked airliner landed in Libya and refuelled. Pregnant woman put off. (Why are planes planes until they are hijacked and then become liners, like ships? Felix shakes his head and reads a notice-board instead.) Ferdinando is beaming at William: 'Domani,' he says proudly. Tomorrow he will have the promised introduction to the Villa Inglese, certainly, without a doubt, he gives his word. Perhaps William will go to Florence today? The coach leaves at ten o'clock. It is a very good coach with air-conditioning also. Felix trots to catch up with William. 'Forgive me, you were asking about the Villa Inglese? Perhaps I can help you there? I am Felix Wanderman – who got your poor wife so wet yesterday. How is she this morning?'

'Fine, thank you. There she is at the window.' Fanny waves. 'You know the Villa Inglese?'

'If Mrs Pottinger is alive I am sure we can arrange something, but perhaps not today.'

'We're going to Florence today,' William says and Fanny calls out to Felix: 'Would you like to come to Florence? We're going today, aren't we, Willy?'

So Felix scampers back to Fra Angelico to get ready for Florence. William sits smoking on the steps outside Bronzino reading the Blue Guide to Florence. From time to time he makes a small neat pencil note. He looks at his watch. It is nine thirty. The coach leaves at ten and he is anxious to board early. In the event of a collision which seats would be the safest? The middle would be furthest from the immediate point of danger in a full-on collision but does he want to be the inside of a sandwich? In any case the most likely accident is a leap from the precipitous road, over which he has no control. William goes back to the Blue Guide.

In Michelangelo Lisa is stuffing her toy-bag. 'For heaven's sake, Jay, people ride on coaches every day. They're like planes nowadays. They have loos and movies and stewardesses. Here, take this.' Jay obediently accepts the Valium but remains unconvinced. He does not fear the coach. To be asked to travel in one is simply as bizarre as if he had been handed a bicycle and told to ride to Florence. (He remembers his first and only bicycle and how he fell off it, having to pretend not to mind. Fat boys are not supposed to mind.)

'Are you ready, Fanny?' Lisa yells across the adjoining terrace but gets no reply because there are delays also in Bronzino. Fanny is ready but Maria of the Smiles has arrived early with her bucket and mop and is not smiling. She nods good morning, bustles around sniffing and sizing up Fanny, decides abruptly that Fanny has the kind of face to which one may confess such terrible troubles, and bursts into tears and a musical but definitely tragic Italian aria.

Fanny smiles as one does, not understanding Italian unless it is spoken very slowly in short sentences, and indicates that Maria must sit down. Giovanni! cries Maria. Mio fratello. Fanny pats her hand and smiles and digs her phrase-book out of her shoulder-bag. Problems and Accidents. A child has fallen in the

water (nell' acqua) – surely not? There is a bus strike. Where
is the police station? Acqua though might be a good idea. She
brings Maria a glass of water. Acqua she says but the aria
is reaching a crescendo, the water is rejected, similarly the
handkerchief for tears. I have missed my train. My luggage is
on board. There has been an accident. 'C' è stato un incidente?'
reads Fanny, hoping that the accent is on the right syllable
(Italian is above all a musical language). Yes, yes, there has
been an incident! Mio fratello, Giovanni, Pisa, macchina. Maria
takes the phrase-book, searches frantically and points: car!
There has been an incident in a car, a traffic accident? Si! No!
Macchina rossa! Bomba!

'Fan? Are you coming? The bus is going. Now!'

Sorry? How do you say sorry?

'Scusi. Molto scusi, Maria. Bus.' But keep the hanky. Fanny
presses the hanky (one of William's large best linen) into Maria's
hand. Maria nods and nods. She has understood bus. The flood
has been at least temporarily dammed but Fanny is not happy
about leaving Maria of the Tears.

'I must just call at reception.'

'There's no time. Hurry.'

To Ferdinando she says: 'Please will you send someone to
our room. Bronzino. There's a woman. There seems to have
been an accident.'

Ferdinando looks up from inspecting his nails.

'Subito,' he says with his dazzling white smile and waves a
hand. 'Have a nice day!'

So now they are settled on the coach. Jay still apprehensive but
soothed a little by the large comfortable seats that recline for
night-travellers, the tinted windows and aircraft-like facility of
nipples for air within easy reach above their heads. There is no
stewardess or sign of a movie but the driver wears an airline
blue jacket and a smart peaked cap. Tickets have been purchased
at reception, the journey will take half an hour and the coach is
only three minutes late departing, having waited for Fanny.

(At the Villa Inglese Daisy Pottinger has finished her breakfast
in bed, been bathed and dressed by her maid. The gardener has

carried her small arrangement of bones to the lounger on the shady terrace and left her with the green telephone that will not ring. No one rings nowadays. Everyone thinks Daisy is dead. Well, there is always something to think about, Daisy says to herself. A good old thumper of a storm last night – quite a lark.)

'What was all that then?' says William, stepping out to give Fanny the window-seat. Fanny looks fussed.

'I don't know quite. I wish I did. It's awful what muddles you get into when you understand a bit of a language. It's better not to understand anything. But something frightful's happened to our chambermaid or rather to someone called Giovanni who seems to be her brother. I couldn't think at the time but that's what fratello means, isn't it? Where's Felix? He might know.'

'Love, you take on too much. You can't help everyone.'

'I know. That's the point. I don't help anyone really. I just left her with your hanky. Let me look in my book. Oh yes, that's it – something has happened in a red car at Pisa. Rossa, you see. Oh, there you are, Felix. I didn't see you.'

The high back of the seat in front has entirely concealed Felix just as the seat has swallowed him. His feet do not touch the floor and he has to sit up very straight to bring his eyes to window level for the familiar but still amazing view.

'Has there been an accident, d'you know?' Fanny explains to Felix.

'It sounds as though there's been a bomba. They seem to have one every day here.'

'I should forget about it,' William says. 'We'll find out soon enough.'

The ride is smooth, the air-conditioning pleasant, the view superb. Everything greener since last night's storm, so that green in all shades and depths has doubled its size and stride and advances on those interesting villas with closed shutters that seem to sleep behind their high gates.

Fanny is soothed by the green, tries to empty her mind of operatic chambermaids and bombs. Lisa is reading Harold Robbins. William, a little dizzy with the intake of information, skips from Guelfs and Ghibellines to the great flood of 1966 and the character of the Florentines which is apparently inturned, insular and tending to the cynical. There is too much here altogether, even for William the eater of books. He wonders if he will ever be ready for the cradle of the Renaissance. But after all there is no hurry. Something has happened.

'What's going on?'

'We've stopped.'

'I know. Why?'

Just below Fiesole but above the Villa Inglese, where the road widens, there is a traffic block. A coach identical to their own but going up while they are going down, has stopped. This is not a drama but a delay. The passengers in each coach look at those in the other coach but all they can see for the tinted windows is the reflection of themselves. Both drivers descend and engage in a discussion in the middle of the road. Are they really reliable? The driver from San Salvatore has taken off his jacket, revealing sweaty armpits, and wears his cap back-to-front. Fanny notices that in the driving cockpit (passengers are prayed not to address the driver in motion), above the steering column, is a spray of small flowers – plastic or immortelles – a crucifix and a photograph, presumably of family, she cannot make out from here. Fanny doesn't mind the delay, she quite enjoys the feeling of movement suspended, but William wants to know what has happened. Jay looks uncomfortable too, since the bus has stopped.

Within the bus theories are exchanged, some quite alarming, but in the end it is Lisa who yawns, pushes Mr Robbins back into her bag and climbs down to find out. From the coach they watch her apparently talking to the drivers, though in what language it is not clear. Fanny wonders if she has misjudged Lisa. Has she really been taking Italian lessons? But she has noticed before – Lisa can make herself understood anywhere, it is part of her job as she circles the globe with Jay.

Lisa is laughing her head off.

'Well, what is it? Why have they stopped?'

'You'd never believe it. That's the coach from the European University and the driver is our driver's brother-in-law.'

'So?'

'That's all.'

Some of the passengers – those who are in a hurry to get to Florence – do not approve. Others regard it as one of those rather charming Italian scenes. It depends on one's attitude to muddle.

The driver climbs back on to the coach. The two vehicles move off in opposite directions freeing the traffic that has built up. Felix puts his head round the back of his seat to speak to Fanny and William.

'There's the Villa Inglese on the left.'

They both turn their heads to look.

'Oh dear! That's where we nearly had the accident, isn't it. It does look beautiful.'

The driver has still not put on his jacket but suddenly remembers his responsibilities and tells them through his speaker: 'We are now leaving Fiesole. Fiesole is an ancient town of many beauties and cool, where the English were often happy.'

Fanny thinks yes, I was happy at Fiesole. We all were.

Air-brakes sighing as it settles on its high wheels, the coach comes to rest with others of its kind nose to tail on the Lungarno della Zecca Vecchia. The passengers too, sigh. Now they have arrived they are responsible for themselves. They must leave their air-conditioned security to find their own way around the gigantic cradle of the Renaissance. Because of the muddle at Fiesole they are late and the coach will depart again for San Salvatore at 17.00 hours. The old hands leave first. They know where they are going. It is airless down here, as though another storm might be brewing and the streets are clogged.

'Phew! Drink,' says Lisa. They had counted on Felix but he has bobbed off to some library and the rest sit in the Piazza della Signoria looking at the Palazzo Vecchio and not knowing what it is. William has his nose in the map.

'What's that, Willy?'

'The Palazzo Vecchio.'

'Are we going to be trippers?'

'Where should we go, Willy?'

'I don't know.' He looks down the list of places not to be

missed for visitors with only a short time at their disposal.

They have another drink and a very expensive sandwich. Lisa says the shops are supposed to be marvellous but where are they? Fanny looks around. She likes the traffic-free square, watching it, the pattern people make as they stand in the midday sun, meet and part, cross in singles or couples or flocks with high-calling guides. Willy is saying Savonarola burned works of art here and then they burned Savonarola. Fanny sees the pigeons walking around their feet, sitting on the head of the statue that Willy says is not really Michelangelo but a copy; she likes the proportions of the square and the relation between the square and the people.

'I don't think there's time to be trippers,' she says, but Willy thinks they could do the Uffizi at least, and then cross the Ponte Vecchio to the Pitti Palace.

Jay looks pale. Where are the taxis? Clearly Jay is not going to make it round any gallery. Today at least the Renaissance will have to do without him.

'What's that green bit,' says Lisa. 'Where it says giardino?'

William looks. 'The Boboli Gardens.'

Lisa likes that. 'Bobbly Gardens.' She decides, 'Jay and I will walk very slowly and sit in the Bobbly Gardens. You can meet us when you've done your gallery and your palace.'

'Well, it's the Uffizi or the Duomo.' William looks worried. And what about the Baptistery? He feels oppressed by the responsibilities of acquiring culture and remembers the picnic with Miss Stimpson and Miss Head with nostalgia as though it had happened a long time ago.

Fanny would have preferred to wander or to join Lisa and Jay in the Bobbly Gardens, or simply to go on sitting here watching the world go by, but loyally she follows Willy. At the Uffizi she would have liked to buy from the stall outside where they are selling rather good reproductions of Leonardo cartoons (the cartoons themselves, she gathers from the notice, are open only to scholars). Inside they get separated – Willy at first going into every room – but he finally catches up with Fanny, planted in front of *The Birth of Venus*.

'Have they restored it? The colours seem too bright, like a postcard.'

The Uffizi is a vast echoing gallery of chambers, a Babel of responses and information in many languages. The American groups are the most efficient, the Spanish the most confusing to Fanny who can hardly take in the Tuscan rooms for the lisping all around her of voices that are not Italian but so bewilderingly close. Now at last she has found a seat and Willy has caught up with her.

'What did Forster say about Florence?'

'He said he was knocked up and he was worried about the starving cats. He kept losing things in shops. But he liked it in the end. Why?'

'I just wondered. There's one lovely Annunciation in a corner. It doesn't look so clever, if you know what I mean. The angel and the lily, but the Virgin really is a girl, surprised.'

'Which Annunciation?'

'I don't know. There are so many.' Fanny ponders. 'I think I prefer the medieval. Except the Bronzinos of the Medicis. Those are fun. So wicked. What time is it?'

'Three o'clock.'

'I'd better go on to the gardens. You catch us up.'

'Are you all right?'

Fanny thinks, I wish people would stop asking me if I am all right.

'Just gallery feet.'

Willy nods. She leaves him in contemplation of Venus simpering.

On the Ponte Vecchio Fanny is not at all sure she is all right. Her bottom is pinched, there is a shouting, a clamour, a press of bodies among those crossing and those coming from the other side, and those around the market stalls. Where is Dante? When was the Arno ever blue? Where are the arm-breaking handbag-snatchers? Where is Italy?

And now the Boboli Gardens are vast, so much more wandering and climbing by high-hedged paths and teasing with closed gardens and vistas and steps promising and then vanishing, it seems impossible that Willy will ever find her here or that she will find Lisa and Jay. Yet it is peaceful and tempts greenly with shade and water: linger, stay. The coach dozing on the Lungarno will soon wake but here after all the climbing is the source of the water-sound: pool and fountain and people resting or walking quietly, children, prams, twined lovers.

As Fanny climbs higher and looks back she thinks, yes, Florence is wonderful but one should take it by degrees, slowly, first as a vista, then a little closer like this, and then at last at its own secret pace; behind the hustle that must be possible? Poor Willy is trying to swallow it all at once. Normally the most orderly sight-seer, he has allowed himself to panic. Lucy Honeychurch in Santa Croce without Baedeker. Willy in the Uffizi with the Blue Guide.

These statues she likes, come upon standing in their niches of stone or topiary as though they had grown there. And now Neptune sporting and puffing in the centre of this basin while at the edge a dove alights on a cherub's head. Someone else settles beside her at the side of the pool. She catches a glimpse of a grubby patchwork skirt. The girl is holding the barefoot baby on her lap, showing it the water.

'Perdita?'

'Oh! Mrs Farmer.'

She looks even thinner, tense as if she might run away.

'How funny, meeting you again. Well, I suppose it's not as you're staying in Florence.'

'I ought to go.'

'Yes, I should too. I'm looking for someone. And then my husband's looking for me. The gardens are much bigger than I realised. Well, Mario's all right.' Mario is in fact irresistible. Unlike his mother, he is a creamy brown. He waves his plump hands at the water, the bird, at Fanny (her arms feel empty; that was how she felt when she left the hospital, Willy so solicitous, Fanny taking it so terribly well. But she wanted to howl: I've left my baby behind). For a crazy second she wonders if Perdita is about to drown Mario, drop him into the water at the edge of the basin face down. An infant that small can drown in three inches of water. Of course not. The girl is holding the baby perfectly safely, she is kissing him.

'He's lovely.' Perdita stands, she puts Mario back into the awful kangaroo pouch. Her shoulders sag. 'It was nice seeing you, Mrs Farmer. I must go.' All around are girls Perdita's age, carefree hand in hand with their boys, girls with books or sketch-pads, girls smiling at their babies, calling their children, the murmur of matrons over prams.

Fanny too stands.

'Perdita, what's the matter? Is something wrong? Hasn't Sergio come back?'

'It's awful. I can't manage. I don't know what to do. But you can't help.'

Fanny thinks, I shall never find Lisa and Jay, Willy is looking for me, we'll miss the coach. But I am involved.

'Do you need money?'

'No, that's all right. Thanks. I've got a bit.'

The girl has already turned away.

'Perdita, wait.' She stands there almost sulky, drooping like Alison. 'You know how to find me. But where are you?'

'That doesn't matter.'

'It might.'

The girl bites her lip. 'All right. If you want. But there's no point.' She dips in her duffel-bag and pulls out what looks like crumpled letters (from the vanishing Sergio?), tearing the top from one and pushing it at Fanny before she turns and runs as though in flight.

The dove on the cherub has flown away. The garden is beginning to empty. Fanny looks at her watch. She must run. No time to find Jay and Lisa now. Will William guess she has gone straight to the coach? The gardens are no longer so attractive as Fanny tries to find the way out. Where are the calm statues? These paths are darker and in places overgrown, a grinning mask gapes water over a crumbling conch-shaped basin, a hideous satyr blocks her way. There is an unpleasant stench – wild garlic?

'Oh! You made me jump.' Fanny nearly screams and then gasps with relief as Felix Wanderman materialises from the ragged topiary.

'Forgive me.'

'No, I'm thankful. I was lost. D'you know the way out? Won't we miss the coach? Did you see me crashing round in that maze?'

'I heard you.' Felix takes her elbow. This is how he first saw her before he knew her: nervous, strung-out. But soon she takes a grip of herself. Felix says: 'There, you see – the Porta Romana. It was only a few yards. And now it's all downhill then across the bridge and a quick walk by the river.'

'I feel such a fool.'

'It's frightening to be lost.'

They are in a narrow street now, almost as busy as the Ponte Vecchio but in a way that seems more benevolent.

'You know Florence well?'

'Not at all.' Felix taps his head. 'A direction bump.'

'But you've been here before?'

'I looked at the pictures while Ada was in the handbag shops.'

'Look, the river's rising. It must have been the storm last night. Poor Jay had his phone cut off. I was supposed to meet them. You haven't seen them, have you?'

'They left this same way half an hour ago.'

'So were you in the gardens all the time?'

Felix nods.

'The library was closed. I've been reading in the shade. Much pleasanter.'

All the same it is a long walk by the river. Fanny looks at her watch again.

'The coach must have gone.'

'Oh no. Half an hour still.'

Fanny's watch has been fast all this time. There had been no need to run. She considers telling Felix about the girl and the baby but she can see, although they are not hurrying too much, the little man is puffed.

'I'm so glad I found you. Or you found me.'

'Fan! You didn't come.'

'Yes I did. But I couldn't find you.'

'Well, we were there. We were there all day.' Lisa looks pleased with herself.

All the same, how did Jay walk all that way?

'Taxi.'

'What taxi?'

But, of course, Lisa would find the only taxi in Florence.

So there they are, all settled again in the coach, everyone exhausted or triumphant or impatient, depending upon their experiences in Florence. But together again, anyway, decisions shed, leather handbags displayed, galleries and museums discussed, restaurants recommended or damned, sandals kicked off, in the relative security of their splendid coach (though the air-conditioning will not work until the engine starts, and the driver is only now climbing aboard). Eyes half-closed, listening, Fanny understands that between them the party has seen half a dozen Florences, every one of which is enthusiastically recommended. Ah yes, but which was real?

'What have you done with Willy?' Lisa says.

'Oh Lord! We were meant to meet in the garden. Are we starting?'

'A minute.'

In the course of whatever happened to him in Florence (the real Florence?) the driver has mislaid his English and Fanny battles to make him understand that they cannot leave without Willy.

'We must wait for my husband. Il mio marito. Tardo.'

Belch, yawn, shrug.

'Troppo tardo.'

The bus is departing at any moment.

Dov 'è William?

The bus will depart now.

Dio mio!

The coach awakes and shudders but does not yet move and there at last is a figure running towards them. The rest of the passengers have not cared to get involved but they are interested to observe the progress of the drama and smile at Fanny as William falls up the steps and through the automatic doors just in time. The upright Englishman is near collapse though he clutches still his Blue Guide, an amulet, a key to the city of Leonardo and Forster and divine beauty and dirty pigeons and bells and coaches nearly missed.

When he can breathe again William says: 'Where the hell did you go, Fanny?'

'Where we said.'

'You said you were going to the Boboli.'

'That's where I was. Waiting for you. Looking for Lisa and Jay. I thought you'd go straight back here but my watch was fast, after all.'

'How did you get back?'

'With Felix. I'm oo oorry, Willy.'

'Felix?' William wants a cigarette very badly but the coach is no smoking. The driver is lighting a cigarette.

'Yes. Everyone seems to have been in the Bobbly Gardens. But we all lost each other.'

William collapses in his seat. Poor Willy. It would have been dreadful to be left behind in Florence. Fanny does understand that (only half an hour ago she felt the same herself) but she is too tired. She is coasting now.

Everyone will feel better soon.

The river, in its brown venomous way, is certainly rising, which to the day-tourists from the hills is a matter of observation but not concern.

The coach is off. The air-conditioning is on.

SIX

In the morning Fanny is shuffling her ever-growing collection of postcards at the bar in the square of San Salvatore. (She has still not written to the children.) The view of the Castello, the Madonna really tearing for the babies and now the cards she bought in a rush outside the Uffizi. The head of the girl with flowers from the Primavera reminds her of Perdita, if only Perdita would smile. So many Annunciations (though not the one she liked best, of the girl surprised). The Leonardo is, of course, wonderful – she is fascinated by the view beyond: steps leading into trees, hills, and is that sea? Simone Martini makes her laugh.

'I'm sorry,' she says, Miss Head and Miss Stimpson are asking if they might join her. 'Of course, please.' Fanny shows them the card: 'the angel looks so mean and the Virgin so cross.' She can't imagine sending any of these cards, but tucking them away like a squirrel, gold against winter.

Miss Head orders tea. Miss Head is probably the only English tourist in Italy who could order tea and get it hot in a teapot with cups and saucers, not glasses, milk, sugar and spoons.

Miss Stimpson ducks her flamingo neck. 'Cissie brought them the teapot the second time we came and showed them how to do it. Did you enjoy Florence?'

'Yes thank you. Though it turned out rather a muddle.'

Miss Head lifts the lid of the teapot to check the contents.

'We had quite a muddle here, didn't we Win?'

Miss Stimpson draws in her neck. Fanny imagines turning her upside down and using her for croquet.

'Oh yes! Frightful!'

'One of the chambermaids lost her brother-in-law. He was a policeman investigating a car at Pisa airport. It blew up.'

'Lost?'

'Well, he was blown to bits, poor man. A red Fiat they seem to think might have been connected with that hijack.' Though her tone is brisk Miss Head is not indifferent. (It was she yesterday who found Maria weeping on the doorstep of Bronzino, got the story from her, calmed her, patted her hand with her own rough brown paw, buttonholed the reluctant Ferdinando and organised everything.) She is aware that the world has become a quite terrible place but continues to look upon its beauties with a strong heart.

Miss Head is not pleased with what she has found in the teapot. 'Teabags again. They never learn.'

If challenged, she would have said that the only view to take nowadays is the short one.

There is Willy coming up the hill. Fanny gathers together her postcards. Only for a moment does she entertain the crazy fantasy of shouting in his face: we inhabit a planet where you open a car door and are blown to pieces. Look!

She thinks of Maria of the Smiles and Maria of the Tears and the red tears on the face of Santa Maria del Castello; and the pure spring from which she had drunk and felt herself in some extraordinary way refreshed beyond understanding, freed to laugh, to weep. A pagan source? It didn't matter. Something old. Now she is away from Art and Florence Fanny can look at her postcards – at the face of Botticelli's ripe spring maiden, Leonardo's gentle girl with her finger still in the page of the book she was reading when the angel brought the astonishing news – and see the faces overlaid each on another – Madonna, maiden, Perdita – so that they shimmer in one vision.

Willy has got over Florence. He took a pill and slept all night like a child with his head on his hands. All the same, he could probably do without Maria of the Tears and the red Fiat and the bomba and what really happened to the brother-in-law Giovanni, which no quantity of red roses can ever heal.

Fanny meets him on the path. They stand hand in hand. Not much of a view. The whole of the Florentine plain is under cloud while here the sun shines, the air is clear.

'I thought I might dig out my paints.'

'Jay wants to go for a spin.'

'A spin?' Now that's another funny old word. Let's be chipper and go for a spin.

'You could take your paints.'

'Why not?'

'Where's Lisa?'

'I think she's gone to reception.'

Jay is beaming this morning. The prospect of a gentle partie de campagne in the Audi has cheered him up.

Felix too is looking rather chipper today, Fanny thinks. He is wearing yellow linen trousers and sporting the red-spotted bow-tie. He raises his sunhat to Fanny. They walk together towards the gatehouse.

'You look smart. Are you off somewhere?'

'Just for a spin, you know.' (In fact, Felix is going to scout out the Villa Inglese, partly on his own behalf, partly on William's. No point in mentioning it, he considers, if Daisy has – as seems probable – dropped off her perch.) 'I might have some good news for your husband tomorrow.'

'Oh, Willy will like that.' Or possibly not, Willy regards all news of any kind with suspicion. He does not like surprises. 'I never thanked you for rescuing me yesterday in the Bobbly Gardens. You always seem to be saving us.'

'A pleasure. It was not so much of a rescue, after all.' Felix tips his sunhat again and trots off for a reunion with his little white car. Fanny watches him pass under the shadow of the gatehouse just as Lisa comes out of reception.

'A nice man.'

'Who? Oh yes. I say, I've been buying postcards. I've found you another Annunciation. You are collecting them, aren't you?'

'Apparently.'

'This one is supposed to have been painted by angels. I must say I wouldn't fancy it much, would you?'

'What?'

'Being told you're pregnant, bingo, and none of the fun.'

Fanny glances curiously at her friend. In Lisa's reflecting sunglasses all you see is yourself.

'Lisa, have you ever been pregnant?'

'Well yes, actually, I have. Twice. Once before I knew you. Once after.'

'That time you said you were going in for a D and C?'

'Fancy you remembering that!'

'I think I guessed. Did you mind? The abortions, I mean?'

'Occupational hazards of a nympho. Yes, I did, as it happens. Or rather, I do now. D'you understand what I'm talking about?'

'Yes, I do. The lost children. What's that? Kingsley? *The Water Babies*? Or *Peter Pan*?'

'You know me. I don't know anything.'

The two women walk slowly up the hill side by side, bare arms touching. Fanny thinks, a friendship can go on for years and years and certain things are said and certain things are not said; intuitions are buried and then one day a truth tumbles out.

'Isn't it silly – I see Sebastian. As if he'd been born alive. I can't talk to Willy about it much, though he's so kind and he'd understand.'

Confessions are easier walking. No need to meet the eye. You might be talking to yourself.

'I didn't know you had a name?'

'Privately, for myself. For him.'

Lisa nods and suddenly grins. 'My mother used to talk about getting pregnant as catching a baby, like flu. If you wanted to I should think Italy's a great place for catching babies.'

'Yes. Italians love babies.'

'I mean if you sit in the sun too long, that bloody angel pays you a visit.'

They have reached the steps to Michelangelo and Bronzino.

'You're coming on Jay's spin?'

'I adore Jay but he can look after himself today.'

'Italian lessons? Lisa, that frightful Ferdinando!'

'Well, he *does* speak Italian.'

Fanny shakes her head, then on an impulse kisses Lisa's cheek. She calls from the steps.

'See you later then.'

Lisa laughs up at her.

'Arrivederci! Ciao!'

Willy is ready.

'What was all that about?'

'Lisa's not coming. She's got her Italian lesson.'

'Has she now? Ah.'

Willy knows. Willy usually knows more than you think he does. Fanny kisses him.

'You're quite sharp, aren't you? In spite of everything.'

'In spite of what?'

Willy has found Fanny's painting equipment and has it ready in the Snoopy bag Alison abandoned years ago and Fanny adopted. Not suitable really at all but she could never quite bring herself to throw it out. She peers inside.

'No, Willy. No Blue Guide today.'

'No?'

'Definitely no.'

Willy is surprised to find himself quite relieved to be guideless.

'We'd better dig out Jay.'

'Mmm.'

As they leave Fanny notices the unmade bed and is reminded sharply of Maria and roses and tears and blood and bombs and Perdita and human responsibility. She closes the door firmly behind her.

So here they are setting out on their mystery tour. Jay has decided to take the wheel for once and is disarmingly pleased to be in command. He changes gear tenderly and is considerate of other traffic. When a donkey and cart appear suddenly before them he idles placidly in neutral. The donkey wears a straw hat with flowers – wilting convolvulus – and a couple in the cart behind on the hay are behaving con amore, more flagrantly than Mr Forster would ever have permitted. No soft glance here but a breast grasped, hands urgently exploring. Fanny riding in front widens her eyes.

'I say!'

Jay smiles benevolently.

'What's that?' William says. 'Why are we going so slowly?'

Fanny grins at Jay. 'Amore.'

'What d'you mean? I can't see. Is something wrong?'

'Nothing at all.' I must not tease Willy, Fanny tells herself. In certain respects he lacks a sense of humour, as would a man who lives on the edge of a cliff. It is unlikely that the man will fall from the cliff but jokes about falling are out of order.

In any case, looking over the boy's shoulder, the girl has seen the Audi, pushed the boy off and buried her face in the hay. Fanny expects the boy to be affronted in his Italian manhood but perhaps that has changed too, for as the cart takes a turning to the left he sprawls on his back laughing and waving. Fanny waves back.

With the road clear Jay changes gear but they still drive sedately.

'Felix has gone for a spin too.' Fanny turns her head to include William, who suddenly remembers.

'What did happen in Bobbly Gardens yesterday?'

'Nothing happened. I got lost and I was found. Where are we going, Jay?'

'I don't know. Where would you like to go?'

'Do we know where we are?'

'No.'

Jay looks rather pleased with himself, out on a spree.

'I keep forgetting if you know Italy. Apart from holidays, I mean.'

They are climbing. The road winds. Jay negotiates a tricky bend before he answers.

'I knew Visconti.'

By midday they reach what appears to be a brown hilltop but reveals itself as the stones take shape to be a village. The sky is white. The heat has burned away colour. Beyond there seems to be a green space among trees suitable for picnicking unless they would prefer to eat in the village. Perhaps first they should find out where they are. The street is empty except for a dog sleeping in the shade and a man walking towards them. They are out of sight of all established landmarks: Florence under cloud, Fiesole, San Salvatore, the chapel of Santa Maria del Castello, the cemetery of the innocents, the vista William shared with Stead and Simpson.

Jay says the engine is overheating, they must stop soon

anyway. They sit in the car. The heat is intense. Flies gather on the windscreeen.

Do we want to stop here? 'How can we know that,' William says, 'until we know where we are?'

'I'll ask.' Fanny opens the door.

'But you don't speak Italian.'

'You'd be surprised.'

The street is nothing but dust. The village is rock. It would be hard to tell where nature ends and man begins. A door bangs although there is no wind. The eyes of the houses are closed to Fanny as she walks towards the man. He wears a white shirt and black trousers. He looks friendly. He is smiling. He carries a camera but has a Mediterranean complexion. In any case there is no one else to ask.

'Dove siamo?' Fanny says.

'Donde?'

William too gets out of the car. Whatever is Fanny up to? Does she need rescue? She is talking to the man and now he is taking a photograph. He peers into the viewfinder and she steps back a little. She is pink with heat and laughing as she gets back to the car.

'Are you all right? What was going on?'

'You'd never believe it. He's Spanish. I don't think he knows where he is either. Lord! It's hot here. Let's go under the trees.'

'But what did he want?'

'He wanted to know where he is. Then he wanted a photograph with me in it.'

'He doesn't know you.'

'Oh, Willy, what does it matter? He just wanted someone in the photograph. He didn't want an empty street. That's all.'

'Peace, my children.'

Jay drives on and parks under the trees. There it is better. They agree it doesn't matter really where they are. A mystery tour need not be a muddle. Whatever buzz of tension there has been between Fanny and William in the car has wasped off leaving no sting. Fanny catches his hand as they look for the best spot to picnic.

'D'you remember how Alison used to hate mystery picnics?

Rob loved them but even when she was quite small Alison always wanted to know where we were going. Seaside or country – she had to know. She made such a fuss once we didn't go at all.'

'I'd forgotten. Alison can be very thoughtless.'

Fanny glances at him, surprised. William is rarely sharp about the children. Sometimes she has wondered if he thinks about them at all.

'Well, she was only seven then.'

It comes into Fanny's mind that although Alison appears to have been cast in a mould so different from Willy's (it is Rob who has his colouring and his gentleness), always scowling with some secret rage, perhaps she is the true daughter of Willy's fears but while he ducks his head she rails at the sky. (When there were thunderstorms in their childhood Rob was normally scared, glad to be comforted, but Alison would shout back, literally, as though to call down the killing bolt: Come and get me!)

No vista here but the water-cool green of the big conifers and the sharper piercing brightness of ambitious infant trees fingering for the sun. Shrubs, a small elegantly proportioned building that might once have been a chapel, half-covered with ivy.

They eat their bread and hard cheese, Fanny and William squatting, Jay amply comfortable in the Roman dining position on a bank that might have been placed there exactly to receive him. 'Perrier?' says Fanny, about to fill Jay's mug but Jay says, 'No. Wine today.' He smiles. Fanny, who can hardly remember seeing Jay without Lisa, wonders if he might possibly be more relaxed because Lisa is not there to protect, to worry, to organise, to remind him by her very presence of the thousand mortal ills and perils it is her job to hold at bay. Faintly dreamy with wine, Fanny sees Lisa, bountiful divine presence armed with arrows on a plump cloud above Jay's head, absent now with that Olympian waywardness in the arms of the frightful Nando. Fanny disapproves but hopes that Lisa is enjoying herself. That is friendship.

'Painting?' says Willy and they dispose themselves around the clearing, Fanny with her sketch-pad propped on her lap (make notes of light and colour and put the wash in later), at the far edge of the picnic spot. She has no false pride. Painting for her is like knitting, although she would like to be better. Meanwhile that nice little chapel or whatever will do very well. She likes the miniature portico, the relationship between the ivy and the stone. She puts on her spectacles.

Perhaps an hour has passed. Fanny realises that steadily the light has been withdrawn and the rags of sky between the leaves are bleached. Jay makes her jump.

'Where's Willy?'

'He went for a walk, I think, in the wood.'

Eaten by giant ants, Fanny speculates, swallowed by snakes. Jay settles his bulk beside her. She covers her pad.

'I'd finished anyway. Phew! It's hot here now. Were you asleep?'

Jay nods.

'I've enjoyed this.'

'Good.'

They sit quietly. Jay says: 'What's been going on?'

'What?'

'Lisa never tells me anything. Something's happened, hasn't it? At the Castello?'

Oh yes. Poor Maria. So Fanny tells Jay about the red Fiat and Maria and the brother-in-law. She almost tells him about Perdita.

Jay nods. 'It's a wicked world, isn't it.'

'Worse, d'you think? Or always the same?'

'Always, I suppose. But we seem nearer to the edge.'

'I think sometimes.' Fanny draws a breath, shakes her head.

'Yes?'

'I think sometimes I would like to believe in the devil. At least that would make some kind of sense. If only we all spoke the same language. Words matter so much, don't they. Is that Willy there? The children are frightened, you know.'

'I didn't.'

'Well. They go on. You know how everyone does at that age. But Rob's friends talk to me sometimes a bit, properly. They really believe that they won't live out the full span of their lives.

There have always been accidents, muddles. Wars, the greatest
muddles of all. But this is different – there's nothing beyond it.
It's not so hard for us. We've had the wonderful things.'

'You have. You and Willy.'

'Yes, we have, haven't we,' says Fanny and she looks up and
there is Willy, walking out of the woods towards them.

Time to go. They pack up the picnic things and painting
equipment. Fanny investigates the interesting chapel and
emerges laughing.

'It's a loo! Absolutely spotless.'

Weird, they agree.

No, Jay is not too tired to drive. Jay wants to drive. This time
Fanny and William sit together in the back seat.

'Well, since we don't know where we are, do we go back the
same way or on?'

'On and down. We can always turn back.'

On then, regardless, wherever.

'Felix! My darling little Felix!' Someone else is chipper today.
Daisy Pottinger and Felix Wanderman sit side by side in twin
lounging chairs on the terrace of the Villa Inglese. He looks like
a small child in a long pram. Daisy was so bored she thought
she was dead. Yesterday's *Telegraph* had not arrived so no
crossword, Grazia had burned the coffee, the hairdresser was
not due until Friday, the chiropodist was away at an international
conference of chiropodists in Pisa, the masseuse who came up
from Florence every Wednesday had sprained her back and
some bomb-people had upset the airport which had upset the
mail, even if anyone had written to her.

And now here is Felix, wearing quite extraordinary yellow
trousers and a red-spotted bow-tie. Ada would die. But then of
course poor Ada is dead. Or poor Felix rather. Daisy knows
what it's like to be the one left behind and everyone else gone
into the darkness with their laughter and their larks and their
kisses and their Daisy-darling-this and their dear-Daisy-that.
Tears. Presents. Jokes. Daisy imagines them all having a party
in another room. Outside the door she sucks her thumb like a
cross child. Let me in. Felix wouldn't know about that. Too

young. Eighty can still gad around. Ninety-seven knows. She pats his hand. What is he on about?

'Foster who, dear? I don't remember a Foster? Potty might have known. He brought clever people. Was Foster clever?'

'E. M: Morgan Forster, the writer. Someone wondered if they could call. You might remember.'

'Oh, bring them ducky, bring them all. Might remember, you never know, a good day. I remembered you, didn't I? Straightaway. Little Felix. Ada was a lovely dancer, wasn't she? Tiny feet. She had the tiniest feet I ever did see. I could tell you now exactly what she wore to a fancy-dress at the Villa Medici. And then it was all gone and afterwards it wasn't the same. Did you know when the fascisti were taking over, Potty had a steel vault dug down there near the potager to put all his pictures in? And covered it up with grass. They never found it. I said, I told Potty, but don't pictures have to breathe?'

Is she asleep? She is breathing. Her head has tipped sideways, her hands ceased to worry the rings Daisy wears on every finger, but the chiffon scarf at her throat still flutters, surely? Felix himself is nearly asleep in the green shade of the parasol. He drifts, dozes, hears Ada call, catches the swish of her skirt at the corner of his mind's eye; she is standing with shoulders bare at the bows of a ship as waves of darkness reach for her. When Daisy speaks he jumps.

'Thought I was dead, didn't you?' She is looking wicked. She has her green eye on him. 'Not now. I mean you nearly didn't come. Kicked the bucket, eh?' Daisy decides to stop teasing. 'Well, I'm ready to go, little Felix. I want to die.'

'Daisy – '

'Not you. You've got your books. But if you hang on too long, you'll see. Snuff myself out tonight if I could. There's Grazia, fat as a pig with a moustache like a hedge. You see. Bringing my damned white wine and seltzer. Be a love, ask for a G and T and swop.'

Felix smiles. 'Anything for you, Daisy.'

'And if you've got a ciggy?'

'Sorry. Don't smoke.'

'Oh well. But you'll bring your Mr Foster? Never see a new

face nowadays. And don't go yet. I want to hear everything. All about Ada, what she's up to.' Felix shakes his head. Grazia of the Moustache arrives with the tray. She either cannot speak English or refuses. Daisy's Italian has always been spasmodic and operatic but somehow communication is established and at last they are alone again looking out over the terraces and the vanished city of gold and noise and rain. The sullen Arno is swelling but here above the cloud they cannot see.

'And what about all these bomb-people?' says Daisy.

'Bomba?' says Felix and they both laugh. Funny word. Bomba.

'Dov 'è San Salvatore? Fiesole? Dov 'è Firenze?'

Fanny sighs. It is possible to ask any number of questions in Italian. Or almost any other language for that matter, given a phrase-book. The problem is to understand the answer. She calls back to the car. 'Willy, where's the Blue Guide? There must be a map.'

'You told me not to bring it.'

'Oh dear. Yes.'

'Let me try.'

Willy tries English. The so-romantic, so-helpful and lovable population of the small hill village has apparently never heard of Mr Forster. Or perhaps they have and are relishing the picturesque muddle as the travellers attempt to communicate that they are lost. An audience has gathered around the Audi, smiling, stroking the handsome bodywork, waiting to see what will happen next. In the corner bar in the shade older men have one eye for football on the television, another for the drama in the square.

Not that it is such a drama. They have the Audi, their womb-like chariot, and the remains of the picnic. And was this not a mystery tour, after all?

Fanny returns to the car. Willy tries French.

'Are you all right, Jay?'

Jay is perfectly happy. He is benign today. He does not even miss his telephone. He does not miss Lisa. He is out on a spree.

'No luck,' says Willy. If there is a real Italy this must be it, but it has its inconveniences.

'Never mind,' says Fanny. 'If we carry on down we can't really go wrong. All roads lead to Florence, then we'll know where we are.'

Willy shudders. 'Do we have to go to Florence?'

'Only to find out where we are.'

So down they go. The road is empty, at least. Down and then up. No need to go to Florence after all.

'The road to Fiesole,' says Fanny. 'We always seem to finish here. Look, there's the Villa Inglese again. And isn't that Felix's car in the drive? Willy, whatever's the matter?'

In the front seat William yelps and claps a hand to his face.

'Willy! What is it? Can you stop, Jay?'

'Not here. Blind corner.'

'Wasp.' William's voice is muffled by his hand.

'Jay, pull in here.'

In Fiesole where the big coaches slumber at midday the Audi comes to rest. Fanny jumps out, opens William's door and unbuckles his seat-belt. Jay says: 'Are you all right, Willy?' Jay does not look too good himself. He should avoid excitement. His stomach is a seismometer for all mortal shocks.

'Willy, take your hands down. How can I see? What was it? Is it still there? Jay, d'you think we're all right here? What does that man want? Why is he waving?' In the midst of her concern for William Fanny sees herself as a character in a phrase-book; as she peels his hands from his poor face and the man in uniform approaches, her mind is a muddle of blood and roses and babies flung from trains and useless accidents of no relevance at all.

'Hornet?' says William.

'No, I'm sure it was a wasp. Where has it gone?' But his face is puffy already, all round his eye which has almost closed.

It could well have been a hornet. William is really being very brave. Fanny tries to think: bicarb for bees and vinegar for wasps? But what about hornets? And which of them can affect the heart? And is Willy allergic? No, that's beetroot and shellfish. A sign says something about parcheggio which sounds like cheese but probably means no parking. The blood has drained from Willy's face and Jay doesn't look much better either. And here is the carabiniere or whatever he is. Fanny remembers Problems and Accidents and Maria of the Smiles in tears in Bronzino.

'Incidente,' she says.

The official is short, poker-faced and polished right down to his snakeskin shoes. Here is the stern father from *Traviata*. His Italian is not to be understood and not jolly.

'Non capisco.' Fanny struggles. She indicates Willy who seems to have frozen in an attitude of pain. 'Il mio marito est malade.'

The official takes out a notepad, searches his pockets for a pen, surveys them all with distaste.

'There is no parking here.'

'I know. Però – ' Or was that Spanish? 'Ma.' If only Willy had lost his luggage or his roses or his baby she could manage.

'This is your car?'

'Si. No.'

'Your licence, please.'

'Dottore! I need a doctor! My husband is fainting!'

'May I see your insurance?'

'Wasp! Hornet!' Oh, for God's sake. 'Vespa!'

'Dov 'è Vespa?'

'There is no Vespa.'

'Then I must have your insurance.'

Another car is drawing up behind them. Someone is getting out. The official is unmoved. He is on the evening shift and missing the football on television. His mother-in-law has come to stay. He cannot sit in his garden. His wife cut his best red roses this morning. His mother-in-law from Milan lost her luggage.

This crazy woman is talking about an incidente. Where is the accident? His mother-in-law's luggage will be in Rome or Naples or Genoa. Tomorrow he will have to telephone Rome and Naples and Genoa. Where is the luggage of my mother-in-law?

'Oh, Felix,' Fanny cries. 'Thank heaven!'

As Fanny and Felix help William up the drive of the Villa Inglese (Jay waits in the car which somehow, miraculously, Felix has liberated) a large insect with yellow stripes circles the head of the policeman as he makes his way back to his office to report an incidente. For a moment the head of the official is bare as he takes off his cap and feels for the bald spot the size of a penny of which his wife reminds him daily. It has certainly spread. He puffs out his chest and replaces his cap. Buzz!

So this is Mr Foster! Of course the impossible husband of Grazia the fat pig will telephone at once for the doctor. There's the sweetest young American in Florence who is a wizard with arthritis if poor Mr Foster would prefer? No? Very well, the local quack. Grazia! Leonardo! Telephone!

'This is really very kind of you, Mrs Pottinger.' Fanny has settled William in the small, cool bedroom, given him two of Daisy's aspirin and returned downstairs, where the extraordinary stick of a woman, who is apparently Felix's friend, is calling for cocktails all round. The cocktails do not arrive but there is an air of festivity as if a party were going on somewhere, lacking only the drink and the guests. The doctor has arrived subito, examined William gravely, sent Leonardo with a prescription and pronounced that the heart-beat is a little palpitating, the eye must be kept covered and in such cases to move for a day or two is not advised. A very nasty sting. Una vespa?

'A hornet, I think.' Fanny is dizzy with relief. She smiles at Felix and Daisy. 'But I couldn't make him understand.' She remembers. 'Oh dear! I must get poor Jay home.'

'Italian policemen are not wonderful,' says Daisy. 'But I insist. Mr Foster must stay. Felix has told me all about him. We always had lots of people when Potty was here, you should have come then. Such fun! Eh, Felix? What have you got to say?'

Felix stands and takes Daisy's hands in his. 'You are as wonderful as ever, my dear.'

Daisy waves her ringed hand vaguely in Fanny's direction. 'Potty popped off, you know. Very dull since then. You must come and see us properly, Mrs Foster, when we're ourselves.'

It has been settled. Fanny feels the decision has been taken out of her hands. She goes upstairs again to kiss William good night but the sedative must be already working, he is asleep.

She kisses his cheek. He looks so peaceful. She could have sworn he was smiling.

Jay has shifted into the passenger seat. He asks after William but clearly it is an effort for him to speak.

'Did you bring your tummy pills?'

He shakes his head.

'We should have got the doctor to look at you. Lisa will be furious.'

Fanny is not used to the big Audi. She tries to drive gently for the sake of Jay's stomach, though it is important to get him back as soon as possible. In her mirror she sees Felix following in his little white beetle. Far below them all sight of Florence is obscured by a gathering of bruise-black cloud.

Daisy's patient opens his eyes and smiles.

So William has arrived, at last, at the Villa Inglese.

SEVEN

They wake to find San Salvatore an ark floating in the sky above a sea of weather. The Apennines have disappeared. There is no Florence, no Fiesole, no Monte Cecéri, and a fine rain falls even on the Castello. Like children told they cannot go to the beach the guests are confused. It never rains at San Salvatore in September yet it is raining again. The universe is out of joint. The coach to Florence is cancelled. There are no coaches from Florence and so no yesterday's newspapers. Only the Japanese arrive from the European University to continue their study of Dante. As they climb from their minibus in the car-park outside the walls of the Castello they raise their faces, the beaks of small birds, to the sky, and unfold from envelope-sized packages fifteen identical grey plastic rain-capes. Wagging their grey wings and discussing either Dante or the weather they pick their sparrow path under the arch, past the gatehouse and up the damp track to the culture hall, leaving behind no footprints.

Tonight they are showing Liliana Cavani's *Portiere della Notte* but meanwhile what to do? The internationally known film director with his harem, the novelists with blocks and the academics on sabbatical, along with most of the population of the Castello, have found their way – many for the first time – to the room which is strictly intended for playing children and furnished accordingly but planned also, according to the brochure, for general recreation of the family.

There are few families here and hardly any children so among the high-tech design rocking-horses, vaginal crawling tunnels and mountain of giant balloon and mattress shapes for bouncing, the guests are gathered with their noses pressed to the picture-window which offers today no panoramic vista, only drizzle.

Someone said once (Jay?), Europe's sinking, they've pulled the plug, and today, Fanny thinks, one could believe that we are the last inhabitants of a continent that has done its time and is returning to the primal sludge, along with the history and the pictures and the battles and the hopes. For one cannot ever, quite, give up hope.

'Sorry? Yes, I hope it will stop.'

The British have come into their own. They are expected to pronounce, as oracles, upon the weather, for it is well understood that is all they ever talk about. Since Fanny and Lisa have let them down, they turn to Miss Head and Miss Stimpson.

'Three days,' says Miss Head. 'Come on, Win, let's buckle on our boots.'

And off they go for a tramp, Heroines of the Weather.

Fanny and Lisa look at the rain.

'God, how awful,' Lisa says.

Fanny has noticed before that rain casts down Lisa unreasonably. Given the sun she can sail through true disasters but under a grey sky her resilience droops. She needs an event. She flumps down on the heap of bouncy play-shapes. 'Wow. Just like a waterbed.'

'How's Jay? I'm sorry we wore him out yesterday. It was rather a chapter of accidents.'

'Stuffed him full of his pills. He'll be fine. What about Willy? Going to see him?'

'Expect so, if I can borrow the Audi.'

The film director is lounging on another of the play-shapes in front of the Sony – the only television in the Castello unless the Marchese has one tucked away in his secret tower. He searches the channels on the remote control and a small audience joins him. There is a choice of an Italian soap opera and two programmes for children, one featuring a talking donkey with rolling eyes and a red hat, the other a talking dog with a revolving tail. The film director's Jackanory girls (as Fanny and Lisa have tagged them) squat at his feet. They look bored. They might have preferred the children's programmes but the film director has settled for the soap opera in which a swarthy lady with a Southfork hairdo is weeping over a bunch of red roses. 'C'è stato un incidente!' she wails. The Jackanory girls play with their hair, yawn and drift away. Then something wondrous happens. They discover the toys. They squeal and giggle in competition for a ride on the rocking-horse. They kick off their sandals to enter the crawling tunnel which wobbles like a drunken caterpillar. One, then two, join Lisa on the heaped mountain of play-shapes and begin to bounce. Lisa bounces. Lisa begins to laugh and kicks off her own espadrilles. Voici! Ecco! Wow!

Fanny waves, see you later, but Lisa is tumbling happily, her big breasts bouncing, among the nymphs, buxom Summer in the company of the daughters of Spring.

Fanny does not feel like bouncing. In spite of William's absence she slept heavily last night and is still thick with dreams, adrift. She could return to Bronzino and complete the line-and-wash of the incredible public loo. She could go and sit with Jay in Michelangelo or seek out Felix in Fra Angelico, his burrow. But Jay will be asleep and Felix will be busy with Christianity. She must, of course, see William – though the idea of handling the big Audi on slippery roads alarms her more than it should. Fanny is a competent driver. It is simply that this morning she lacks will as if her spirit had been sucked from her, and so she wanders in the rain around the Castello. San Salvatore floats above the darkest clouds, occasionally there is even a shaft of pale and watery sun but the rubbish-tip smells, the rain has emptied the secret gardens and the hedged paths, the playground is no longer enchanted. Fanny's mind wanders to the notes of intercession laid at the skirts of the dusty Madonna up the hill. Sebastian, she thinks, keep him in peace, and presses her hands to her eyes.

'Missis? Missis Farmer?'

Fanny is at the gatehouse without any idea of how she got there, and the frightful Ferdi is calling. Ferdinando will not get wet so Fanny must enter.

Ferdinando is slipping a comb into his shirt-pocket, having rearranged his greasy coiffure. Today he is wearing a Hawaiian play-shirt.

'Hello, Ferdinando.'

'You are having a nice day, Missis Farmer?'

'Not particularly.'

'I have a message for you. Most urgent.'

Willy?

'My husband? Is my husband all right?'

'Oh yes! This is a young lady who says she has trouble. Perdita. I have her name.'

'Perdita? Is that all she said? Ferdinando, this is very important. What else did she say?'

'Nothing. That is all. Trouble. Perhaps un incidente? When she was saying more she put down the telephone. This is a friend with trouble? Missis Farmer, where are you going?' Fanny is at the door.

'Have a nice day!'

Fanny stands in the rain. Misses Head and Stimpson are emerging from Giotto buckled into their boots and wearing enormous rain-capes which Miss Stimpson carries off with a certain style.

Miss Head beams. 'What a bucketing! Let's hope the Madonna's doing her stuff.'

'Madonna?'

'Santa Maria del Castello in the cappella up the hill. She's supposed to save San Salvatore from flood. Saints preserve us, eh?'

'Oh yes?'

Miss Stimpson shoots out her head on its long neck from under the visor-peak of her rain-hat.

'The Arno's rising, you know. Poor things, I hope they don't get cut off. They had a frightful time in 1966. Such a funny little river, you'd never think it, would you?'

'Come along, Win. Miles to go before we sleep!'

'Coming Cissie.'

Off they stump and Fanny watches them go. Twenty minutes later sitting by William's bed in the Villa Inglese she is accepting a brandy from Daisy Pottinger's Grazia of the Moustaches.

'I'm sorry. So silly. Not used to the Audi, I suppose, and the road's slippery. Just a skid. The car's all right.'

'But are you all right, my dear Mrs Foster?'

'Oh yes, much better now.'

The room is small. Daisy hovers and William sits up looking fresh and oddly youthful in the Napoleon bed. Apart from the swelling his skin has a boyishly pink hue. When Fanny entered she had the feeling she was interrupting.

'Are you sure, love?'

'Yes, I'm fine now, really. But what about you?'

Daisy is perched like a small, thin, smart cat on the edge of a straight-backed chair. Her jewelled fingers flash in the dim room. She wears a green chiffon scarf at the neck and a bounce of short curls that Fanny guesses can only be a wig. Clearly she is thrilled with Willy and he with her. He has always been good with old ladies. In fact, Fanny has the impression that William is having a ball.

'The quack-quack says Mr Foster must stay in bed for at least another day.'

'Oh dear, I'm sorry we're being such a nuisance.'

'Nuisance? Nonsense! If you knew, Mrs Foster. Ninety-seven is being bored. Don't get too old, I advise you. It's tiresome.'

'Actually, it's Farmer. Fanny Farmer.'

'And when I remember, I've promised to tell your nice husband all about Mr Morgan the writer. Potty would have known. There were all kinds here in those days until the fascisti came. I liked shopping better, and parties.'

'You have a beautiful house.'

'They changed the name, of course, those fascisti, and we had to run away. But it was still the Villa Inglese. Well, we mustn't tire Mr Foster, must we.'

I'm being chucked out, Fanny realises. The brandy has gone to her head. She could laugh or cry. She looks at William. Will he ask her to stay? He smiles.

'I'm not happy about you driving back.'

'Oh, I'll be fine.'

'Take care then.'

'You too.'

Fanny kisses William, aware of Daisy's seagull eye. Outside the door, on the landing, Mrs Pottinger dismisses her.

'Sometimes I think things are intended. Don't you? Accidents can be blessings.'

'I'll call tomorrow, thank you. If I may.'

'You look peaky, my dear. You're sure you wouldn't like another little brandy? We could all have a little brandy?'

'No, thank you. Really. I'm fine.'

I'm fine, Fanny tells herself, walking in the rain up the hill to Fiesole. She tried to start the car several times and only grasped after her third attempt that the Audi had run out of petrol at the gates of the Villa Inglese.

She should find a garage. She should telephone Lisa. She could get a taxi back to San Salvatore and let someone else cope. Instead, in a Fiesole she barely recognises, punished by rain, golden leaves sodden, trippers dripping glumly, at the outdoor bars chairs tipped up against tables, Fanny sits in a narrow indoor café. She is the only woman. On the television slung above the bar football is being played somewhere else where the sun shines. The grass is green, the players weave and kick and kiss in the small sun-baked arena under a hard blue sky.

Someone has left a newspaper on the table which sports also a single red plastic rose in a miniature Perrier bottle. *La Nazione*. Fanny understands the headlines. A bomba has been discovered in the Vatican. There is early snow in the Apennines. A military jet has crashed. She tries to read the text which she understands and does not understand. It is a cryptogram, yielding frustratingly several words in a sentence but never the structure that might make sense of it all. Prima Linea – a football team or a terrorist group? A picture of the Pope on his knees kissing some unnamed piece of earth, the wind blowing up his skirts. Have they blown up the Pope? Surely they would not be watching football if the Pope had been blown up? Then lower down a shot of a landscape of thin snow and dirty scraps of metal, a lopsided wooden cross and a scattering of roses, grey in the newsprint against the dirty snow.

'Signora?'

'Si. Un caffè.' What was black? 'Nero, per favore.'

That flick of the eye that might be laughter or contempt.

'One black coffee.' The waiter's accent, to Fanny's ears, is the most delicate parody of English. He flicks her table with the corner of the cloth he carries over his arm, returns to the bar, gives the order and starts a lively conversation with his cronies round the television set – his only sign of animation so far. There is laughter. Are they talking about the football? No. Heads turn to appraise Fanny. She catches a glimpse of herself in the mirror: hair frizzed with damp, the old Laura Ashley dress she put on this morning creased and soaked at the hem. Wild middle-aged woman in girl's party-frock. After Daisy's generous brandy she ought to ask for something to eat but she sips her coffee, which is acid. A girl with an infant in her arms comes into the bar, laughing at the rain. She is Italian, she is known, a daughter or a granddaughter. The baby reaches for the plastic roses in the jug on the bar and doting Grandma plucks one out for him while the daughter laughs and flirts and coos and kisses. There comes to Fanny a cold, dull thought, bleak as a stone: there should have been flowers for Sebastian. He had lived. Behind the backs of the softly worrying nuns, with all the pain, she had known the moment the foetal heart had stopped but she had not cried out, she had not wept until the day with Felix at the spring.

The cathedral campanile tells Fiesole it is midday. From her seat in the bar Fanny sees the bus arrive from Florence. On television they are no longer playing football. The commentary is beyond her.

What stories are the visual images telling? There is the Pope again getting up from kissing another blessed piece of airport earth, waving from his Popemobile, kissing babies, beaming, enjoying it all like an actor. People are throwing flowers at the Pope. He appears to be in one piece. There is the wreck of the plane in the snow. The Arno (in 1966?), Santa Croce awash. But that cannot be today for the bus from Florence has arrived at Fiesole.

And now what's this? An airport. A British airliner shaking in the heat. The same plane taking off into a sky of purest blue. Another airport: Pisa. The jagged remains of what might once have been a small red car. Bomba says the newsreader and continues to talk as two stills come up with captions. A youngish policeman: Giovanni Ghirlandio, followed by what can only be a mug-shot of a scowling boy with curling brown hair: Sergio Dolci. These last images are all apparently linked and Fanny feels she is on the edge of making the connection, she knows she is connected with this picture-world of danger. But if this were the Giovanni of chambermaid Maria of the Smiles, and Perdita's Sergio, what is that to Fanny, sitting in a bar at Fiesole remembering the road from Pisa to Florence in the rain in a red Fiat and another red Fiat driving too fast in the other direction? And Perdita drooping and lost by the basin in the Bobbly Gardens, then the message this morning: trouble.

She has not come to Italy for trouble and muddle, she has come – as have they all at the Castello – to shed responsibility, not to assume it. She could pay for her coffee, walk out of the bar into the rain, take a taxi up to the Castello and let someone else deal with the problem of the Audi incapacitated in the drive of the Villa Inglese. She could look for a garage. She could apply for help at the Villa Inglese. She could at least have a sandwich while she makes up her mind.

'Signora?'

Damn the man. Digging in her handbag for the money to pay, Fanny finds a scrap of paper, an address torn from a letter of which only one word remains: Cara. It is a pathetic, thumbed and crumpled shred of life as small as those telegrams of grief and supplication at the feet of Santa Maria del Castello, but it settles the matter for Fanny. She flings some coins on to the saucer, runs out into the rain and jumps on the bus returning to Florence just as the doors are closing. She says to the driver, Firenze, and pays. He is annoyed. Everyone else seems to have a ticket already and Fanny remembers from William's Blue Guide that tickets of a set price may be purchased to take you anywhere. She likes that idea: a ticket to anywhere.

While the bus coming up was full, very few people seem to be going down to Florence today, so Fanny actually gets a seat on the small bus. She is aware how wild she looks – no coat since she had expected to drive the Audi to the Villa Inglese and return the same way. But the bus is better than the bar. She is the only tourist. There is the feeling of a small band of travellers making a potentially dangerous journey. As the rain outside thickens and they pass through cloud, the grandmother opposite leans forward, taps Fanny's knee and points upwards. Heaven or rain, what does she mean? Fanny smiles. It doesn't matter. And so they sway on down, neither in flight nor pursued, in the rain, in blessed limbo, somewhere between heaven and hell, on life's passage from one awakening to another sleep.

'Oh yes,' says Daisy. 'Sometimes I forget if Potty had sugar in his tea but when I was a girl with my mother I heard them talking about the Via dei Bardi. A Mr Crust? Or Cussed? Funny name. Arty sort of tea-parties, can you imagine it? All men! What could they find to talk about? But perhaps your Mr Morgan was there. Then there was I Tatti later. The further back things are the better I remember them. But I can't tell you much about I Tatti. We went there, of course – Potty and his pictures – but it was a dull sort of place, I thought. I once dropped off in the middle of what was supposed to be an interesting party. Nose in my champagne, snoring, Potty said. I never snore, I told him, only men snore, everyone knows that.'

So Daisy runs on and William hears and does not hear her, in the same way he is vaguely aware of the rain outside. Here he is tucked up in the Napoleon bed in the Villa Inglese yet he no longer finds himself so interested in looking for Mr Forster. Perhaps he has lived too long with his secret project, the monograph on Forster in Italy, pictured too often this moment when he might come upon new unknown material. Now it is his, he has only to reach out and grasp it, the booty has lost its glitter.

Yet he is happy, of lighter heart than he can remember being for years. He welcomes even his swollen aching face, in retrospect he welcomes the hornet whose sting may at least for the moment have averted the killing bolt from a heaven so bewilderingly full of spite. What have we done, he wonders often, that demands such expiation? Simply to be born seems to be to step into mortal peril. All he can hope – and he does so fervently – is that Fanny too might be blessed with this remission.

Thus William floats, in this Imperial bed intended for battle, one eye closed tight, nursing his wound and relishing this holiday from life. With the other eye he notes that Daisy has dropped off, head on one side like a bird on a branch. And as the carriage clock strikes the midday, she wakes as if she had merely been interrupted in the middle of a sentence.

'Oh good! Time for drinkies, don't you think?'

At San Domenico the bus coming up from Florence passes the bus coming down. Fanny's bus almost empties. The drivers are shouting a conversation. What are they saying? The greenery of the heavenly villas is heavy and dark with rain. The grandmother taps Fanny's knee again.

'Alluvione.'

'Si. Yes. Thank you. Grazie.'

Wrong answer, apparently. Granny shakes her head. She points down. Hell? The rain is so heavy now it is impossible to see more than the shaking images of the passengers in the ascending bus. And that must be how they see us, thinks Fanny, light-headed from cognac and coffee. How queer. She smiles. She wants to tell someone how funny it is but Granny wags her head again. She wouldn't see the joke.

At the stop at the Piazzale Michelangelo the famous panorama has been washed away. Nothing to see. No Duomo, no Firenze, no Arno, no Pistoia, no peaks of the Apennines. What a pity, Fanny thinks, the journey's nearly over, below awaits responsibility.

As the bus starts up again she rummages in her bag. No guide, though there is a postcard map of Florence she bought for the children (who would not be interested) and did not send (but one should send, one should never stop sending), no phrase-book, but Fanny does find the torn-off address and offers it hopefully to Granny along with the postcard map.

'No.'

'No?'

It is a bad address? It does not exist? It does exist but it is a bad address for even as she traces the map with her blunt forefinger Granny is wagging away again. Off the map, apparently, north-east of the centre and then, as Granny explains very slowly as if talking to an idiot but so that Fanny can get the sense, one is on one's own.

As the bus crosses the Arno Fanny looks down and sees that the muddy trickle has grown up; it has become a real river of whirls and currents, boiling, spiteful, grabbing at the land.

By the time they reach the Duomo she has made up her mind and stands ready at the door for getting off which is never to be confused with the door for ascending. Standing in the rain there she has an alarming but exhilarating conviction of something having been decided. Very well then. So be it. Off the map.

Back at the Castello, others have discovered the pleasures of the playroom. A white-haired, distinguished Nobel prize-winner in purple track-suit and a German art historian in khaki shorts are playing pig-in-the-middle with a big orange ball and a short lady novelist from Highgate who knows more about Ivy Compton-Burnett than anyone else in the world and stamps her foot each time the ball eludes her. She doesn't stand a chance. Nor does the continental film director whose nymphs, refusing to respond to his call, continue their bouncing and squealing. He sulks. On television the children's programmes and soap opera have given way to football on all channels. A middle-aged Dutch couple, having watched the games at first with astonished disdain, are now shyly taking it in turns on the slide. Ock! they cry each time they land on the mattress.

Jay, feeling better, has found a golf-umbrella in the closet and come to look for Lisa. At the door to the playroom he finds a small child sucking its thumb. Wide-eyed, they both watch the grown-ups playing.

The bus from Florence – much fuller than Fanny's going down – has arrived at Fiesole. Everyone, it seems, is running away from the flood or the threat of flood. There is a rumour that this may be the last bus from Florence. Some descending are immediately embraced by family and carried away, others make directly for hotel or pensione and the rest fill the bar nearest to

the bus-stop. Only one figure is left standing: a girl without a
coat, carrying a well wrapped bundle. She seems to be looking
for shelter. The bar is packed and she appears, in any case,
disinclined to enter. She tries the Cathedral but it is closed until
three o'clock. She sits for a moment on the Cathedral steps,
her body hunched, shielding the bundle, then sets off, still
bowed, up the hill. Is that rain on her face? Or tears? As she
climbs little traffic passes her, only two minibuses – Germans
going up, Japanese coming down.

'Ospedale? Hospital?'
    'Si. Ospedale.'
Before she went off the map Fanny should have had something
to eat. Instead, clutching her scrap of paper, she wandered for
a moment aimlessly in the area of the Duomo and found herself
caught up in a sodden Babel of trippers, one of several around
the Baptistery, daring all for a glimpse of the Gate of Paradise.
Dripping from their peaked hoods, they surrounded Fanny,
carried her along, obedient to the shrill call of the guide. La
porte du Paradis! Elbows nudged her. Porten til Paradis! Her
foot was painfully needled by an improbable high heel. She felt
faint, dizzy, pushed from behind in the direction of the great
doors and at the same time thrust back. Mi scusi. Sorry. Je
m'excuse. Die Tür des Paradies! Hey folks, over here! Can't
you look where you're going? You with Unitour? Sorry!
    And then off the map it was another Florence, of narrow
streets that seemed to turn back on themselves then empty
suddenly into squares that led back to the same streets. The
rain had drawn out an awful stench, everything rotten in the city
was breathing; only youths were abroad in a few of whose faces
Fanny thought she could just perceive through a curtain of rain
Leonardo's thyroid, androgynous angels. Dov 'è? she said. The
youths had gone, the shops were closed, in grim drinking-places
the backs of old men were turned against her. A dog followed
her for a street or two, one eye blind with cataract, its coat
naked in patches as if someone had been rubbing and rubbing it
off.
    Then a guarding angel, a cemetery, a grave heaped with new

flowers and a curt priest gave directions to the mad foreign woman with her scrap of paper and her dov 'è. So now here she is confronting the grandmother of Mario who does not speak English and has her own problems besides.

Before stepping down into the dim wine-shop Fanny has armed herself: I'll bat the old cow if she doesn't tell me. If I can make her understand. Santa Croce without Baedeker is not Dolci's wine-shop without phrase-book. But there is no immediate difficulty, simply a scream to the back for someone to serve another customer and for Fanny a shrug. Fanny feels she might get further by asking for Mario rather than Perdita. After all, this must be Signora Dolci and Mario must be her grandson. The woman screams again to the back room and admits that Mario has gone to the Ospedale. She seems incurious about Fanny's motive though her sharp Florentine eyes take in the strange appearance of Fanny herself, a middle-aged foreigner soaked to the skin in a child's dress.

Fanny struggles on.

'E Perdita?'

'Spedale.'

But where? Again dov'è, always dov'è. The answer yet another shrug and Fanny is dismissed. The broad back is turned. Italians do not always love babies.

One of the Leonardo urchin-angels is kicking a can in the street. Eyes shining as he lights on his victim.

'You want something, Missis? Handbag?'

'Si. Hospital. Ospedale.'

'No handbag?'

'No. Hospital.'

'Ospedale. You come.'

He nips in front, running back every so often to make sure she is following through the maze of streets that lead eventually to a part of town Fanny recognises. So it is that Fanny finds herself at four o'clock in the afternoon not in a hospital of small white cots but by a misunderstanding that is very understandable, back in the real Florence of the tourist in the Piazza Santissima Annunziata gaping at the Spedale degli Innocenti and the sad della Robbia foundlings in their swaddling clothes. Against the blue background their arms are spread in an attitude almost of crucifixion. Looking for life, she has found art.

The first bar has no seats. In the second she sits over a brandy trying to chew the dry little sandwich. How do you find a baby in this country of babies? (I left you at the hospital, Sebastian, they wouldn't let me see you but I saw your face today in stone.) On the wall there is a poster: San Salvatore. Festa della Santa Maria del Castello. Under cover of mopping her face she dabs her eyes. I'm at it now: tearing for the babies.

'Telephone?' she says and buys her gettone. She still has in her handbag the brochure for the Castello, with the number.

'Lisa?'

'Hello? Who's that?'

'Lisa, I can hardly hear you.'

'Fan! It sounds like water on the line. Gargling. Are you gargling?'

Fanny rests her arm against the wall and her forehead on her arm.

'No, I'm not gargling.'

'Are you at the villa?'

'What did you say?'

'How's Willy?'

'Lisa, listen. I'm in Florence.'

'I can't hear you at all. You'll have to shout.'

'Lisa?'

'Damn it, we've been cut off.'

Gurgle. The Arno is still rising. Will the beautiful pictures be lost? Fanny squishes along the Lungarno. There is a dead fish. The bus for Fiesole is not departing. There is no taxi. There are not many taxis in Florence and today they will not go to San Salvatore or even to Fiesole. The sky in Italy is not blue. Fanny does not have a blow of the sun. She has a badness of the gullet. Doctor, my heart has pain. Here is the white minibus of the nuns! I have to go to San Salvatore. Do you go to Fiesole? Do you speak English? Parla italiano? Parla francese?

The old-fashioned wimples wag and smile. Fanny is pressed gently into a seat. She could be drowning in a cloud of doves.

What language are they speaking? She has never heard it. It could be a language someone has invented. There are no clues. In the hospital the nuns used a foetal doppler to tell if he was still alive. To discover he was dead, as she could have told them. Foetal doppler? What are you talking about? What language are you speaking? Herr Doppler, what is the foetal status? Language is funny. You have dreams like this. You dream that you can speak a language you have never heard. You dream of faces you know speaking a language you do not understand. Is she asleep? Does she know she is dead?

Fanny is helped carefully from the bus. She looks up and sees the wall of the Castello, toppling against a high moon and running clouds, and beyond that a starless sky and endless, endless night.

EIGHT

'Steady, Fan. Drink up.'

'What? What's wrong?'

'Nothing. The doctor's coming.'

'I don't want a doctor.'

'Look, love, drink this. Jay, you try.'

'Fan darling. Come on.' Kinder hands or simply softer hold a glass of lemony water to her lips.

'Jay?'

'That's right. Now rest. Close your eyes.'

'So tired.'

Except for the cough and the tightness in the chest it is a not unpleasant sensation to be as a child again entirely suspended from responsibility. Drink, say the friendly and familiar voices, sleep. Dreams are wild and dangerous. Fanny wakes gasping and sweating but keeps her eyes shut. If I stay very still all will be well.

'Shush.' She is at Rob's bedside. Willy is frightened to come into the room in case his children die. 'That's lovely.' Someone is mopping her forehead with a moist sponge. Fanny has lost a baby. 'Where's baby?'

'Who, Fan?' Lisa murmurs to Jay: 'Oh Lord, is she delirious? Does she mean the one she lost? Poor love. What was she doing in Florence anyway?'

Jay doesn't know. No one knows. Daisy Pottinger telephoned from the Villa Inglese to say the Audi had been found in the drive out of petrol. Leonardo would get it filled and bring it up to the Castello. She'll just tell William that Fanny has a little cold, all right, ducky?

Jay is like Nana in *Peter Pan*, a big gentle dog guarding Fanny's sickbed. He has found a new role and will not listen to Lisa or take his medicine. For two nights he refused to go to bed but sat up in Bronzino while Fanny rambled and coughed and sweated. In his concern for her he has forgotten his telephone and his tummy. He tends her in ways you would think only a woman would. He has changed in some marvellous way, or perhaps he has simply seized the chance to change. He sends Lisa away and sits in Bronzino by one small lamp, listening to Fanny's breathing. He dozes. At dawn Fanny is breathing more steadily. Jay looks through the books on the night-table. William's Forster, Luciano Berti's *Florence* and on Fanny's side an Italian teach-yourself book with a card stuck in a page. He reads: There was once upon a time (c'era una volta) a peasant woman who had a hundred sheep, twenty-eight cows, fifty-five pigs, nineteen goats, a dog and a cat, and she was very happy. Jay has hardly read for years. He has people who read for him. For a second he is returned to the innocence of story, wondering what will happen next.

For two days Daisy Pottinger's quack could not come subito because the storm had brought down a tree blocking the road from Fiesole, so they cannot be sure what is wrong with Fanny, even where she has been, though Lisa found a Florence address in her handbag. The doctors among the guests of the Castello can offer only philosophy or literature. Cut off by the weather and the fallen tree from news of the real world, the community is feverish with rumour. The flood has reached Santa Croce, rats have run wild from the sewers and there is talk of cholera in Florence, the return of ancient plagues. The olives are spoiled, the festa will be called off; it is not such fun to play any more. Sometimes the television works, sometimes it does not. The hijacked plane has landed at Geneva but the terrorist has escaped. The plane has been blown up. The terrorist has escaped by parachute. The terrorist, disguised as a woman, has left the plane with other passengers. The weather has pinned down the yellow helicopter of the Marchese but police have infiltrated San Salvatore disguised as nuns. The airport is closed. The coach does not run even to Fiesole. The terrorist is dead. The terrorist is not Sergio Dolci, not a member of an

Armenian splinter group but a son of Islam. The Marchese was responsible for the Vatican bomb-plot. The Marchese who might have enlightened them, is silent in his tower. The Marchese has fled to Greece. The rain has caused the drains to blow back (that, at least, is true) and there is an epidemic of stomach trouble. Wherever two or three are gathered together bowels are the subject of intense debate, the Castello more or less equally divided between starvers and dopers.

The atmosphere in the Castello is of a city under siege. Everyone is nervy. They have real lives to go back to, they tell each other, they must become again academics, novelists, cellists, art historians, critics, film people, telly people, philosophers and ornithologists. How would the world get on without them? (Pretty well.)

'Honestly,' Lisa says, 'you'd think they all had a train to catch. I suppose some of them have.' Lisa herself takes her role seriously but she can see the joke. 'Oh Lord, the trots again!'

Lisa, Jay, the Misses Head and Stimpson and Felix are among the half dozen eating in the refectory. Fabrizio has stopped performing since there is no one, in his view, worthy of his performance. He cooks, leaves the rest to his underling, and retires to sulk.

'Three days,' says Cissie Head. 'You see. Silly fuss. It'll all be over tomorrow.'

Miss Stimpson blushes and offers daringly: 'All the same. One can understand. Sometimes, Cissie, I think you're rather hard. One shouldn't expect more of people than they can give. Don't you think, Professor Wanderman?'

'I expect you're right.' Felix bobs his head. He has difficulty eating because the humid atmosphere mists his spectacles. He wishes Ada were here. Ada always had an opinion. The mood of daring which had seized him at the start of the holiday has for the moment deserted him. He no longer sports the spotted bow-tie. He spurns his heart pills still but feels rebuked rather than euphoric by the sight of the little brown bottle in the bathroom cupboard. It is not entirely the weather. He has been aware of a lowering in his spirit ever since the visit to the Villa Inglese. Seeing Daisy (finding her alive) has in some way shaken him, reminded him of his own mortality. The Daisy he had held in his mind all these years had been a creature so far from this bundle of dying bones, he shivered to think of her. Yet the essence, the Daisyness of Daisy was there still – it was the poor flesh he could not bear to witness. At funerals he had seen the glint in the old survivor's eye but this encounter was worse than any burying. Daisy, clinging to the fragile edge of life, looked at Felix from the grave.

Those who run the Castello (it is never quite certain who does run the Castello – surely not Frightful Ferdinando), maybe observing the mood of the guests, have laid on a treat tonight: Visconti's *Death in Venice*. Lisa is elated. Even Jay is persuaded to leave Fanny sleeping. The continental film director takes a double dose of Lomotil. His nymphs flank him, demure as schoolgirls before this great cultural experience. Even the Misses Head and Stimpson attend. Miss Stimpson is puzzled by the pleasant scent of marijuana. Miss Head is not. With queasy stomach Felix watches – not the only one in the cinema to feel that art can at times come uncomfortably close to life. Of course the rumours from Florence are absurd, of course there is no parallel at all, but all the same there is a more than usually sharp frisson as poor Aschenbach makes his decision to stay in the doomed city. Afterwards no one lingers for a chat. Lisa runs through the rain with more urgency than ever to the arms of Nando. Felix returns to his burrow and a sleeping pill, Miss Head and Miss Stimpson to cocoa in Giotto. Night falls on the Castello, on Lisa thrashing in the arms of Ferdinando, on Felix's dreams of Ada's laughter, Daisy's face and an open grave, on the campers huddled in their dark tents outside the walls watching the lights of San Salvatore go out, one by one.

In the morning the rain has stopped, the tree has been cleared from the road, the Castello has woken to a watery sun and the arrival of the doctor. Hardly subito but efficient if monolingual.

He is brisk with the plaintive victims of the plague. Acqua minerale and niente to eat. He sighs. He is tired of tourists. He loves his country and would have liked to have it to himself. This is not a good day. It is his wedding anniversary and he has forgotten to buy red roses for his wife. If he buys them now she will throw them out of the window.

With Fanny he spends more time. Having examined her he draws himself up to his full five and a half feet and fires a volley of Italian questions at her.

'I'm sorry, I don't understand. Lisa, pass me the phrase-book.'

Fanny and the doctor study the phrase-book (Seeing the Doctor: subdivision of Problems and Accidents) and determine that Fanny does not have, in alphabetical order: an abscess, an allergy, appendicitis, asthma, constipation, diarrhoea, hay fever, headache, indigestion, insomnia, stomach-ache. She does have an ache, cold, cough and sore throat.

The doctor pronounces: 'Pleura.'

Whatever's that? Sounds like tears. Not in the phrase-book. Fanny ponders.

'Pleurisy?'

The doctor is pleased. He positively beams. Si, pleurisy. But now, he indicates, it is finished. He wags his finger. Fanny must take precaution. He frowns, digs in his bag and sternly presents her with a bottle of pills. Fanny nods. She understands. He is pleased again. He shakes hands with everyone and trots off, to buy roses.

'Well, that's all right,' says Lisa. 'Swallow your elephant pills and if you're good you can get up.' She fills Fanny's glass with mineral water. 'Oh, by the way, Nando said someone was looking for you the night of the storm. Very late. He said you were ill and she went away.'

'Who? Lisa, this is important.'

'Just a girl. She looked a bit crazy, Nando said. Does it matter?'

Fanny shakes her head. No point in explaining. But left alone, she considers the strangeness and contrariness of it: Perdita coming up the hill while Fanny was making her mad dash down to Florence. How their paths must have crossed yet they failed to meet. They were probably within three yards of each other on their separate buses but Perdita and Mario might just as well have been invisible. It is like one of those fairy stories in which people seek one another in a forest, come upon tracks, embers of a campfire, a scrap of torn clothing, a sign, false trails, a mark on a tree; they hear a voice call, a twig crack but meetings are always just missed or forestalled. Accident and magic intervene. Or it may be an Italian muddle. Or life, the witch who sets brambles and thorns between us and those we love, so we misunderstand, see them fade before our eyes when we most want to catch their hands; sometimes there is a temptation to retreat from the whole hazardous enterprise.

Fanny thinks of William. Believing their love to be strong and sure, she wishes all the same that it were possible to carry it for renewal and refreshment to some magical spring (she may have hoped for something of the sort of Tuscany yet here they are tucked up in separate beds, in the Villa Inglese and San Salvatore). And then, of course, the children. Ah, the children. What a muddle there! For so long Fanny has felt if only I could find the password, it is my fault, it is their fault, they have changed, I have not changed enough, the face of Sebastian (never seen) has clouded my vision, the golden child, the lost one, while they are most urgently alive and in need. It is not something to be reasoned. Standing before the mirror, dressing slowly, weaker than she expected, Fanny receives one of the odd unlooked-for messages that arrive most often between waking and dream and then are gone and rarely make sense: simply love, that is enough.

Just as Fanny takes her first uncertain steps the sun returned is awakening others from panic, illness or mere boredom. Even Willy rises from his bed in the Villa Inglese (Daisy protesting) and takes a look at his face in the mirror. The swelling has gone down but his eye is still fiercely inflamed. He is undecided. He wants to see Fanny (the mystery of the abandoned Audi in the drive has been kept from him) but on the other hand Daisy could be right, it would be foolish to take risks. Just one more day, perhaps, on the terrace in the sun? Daisy's little drinks, Daisy's tempting little snacks. Daisy has suddenly and temporarily got her memory back. She thinks she might even lay her hand on correspondence between Potty and Forster. And she remembers him now, oh yes, quite well, but a funny nothing-much sort of man who looked like a mole and was pecky about his food. On the companion lounger on the terrace William listens and does not listen. Here is the treasure he has sought so long and now it no longer interests him so much. Daisy chatters on and William pretends to listen, knowing this to be a unique opportunity, given only to him, it will never come again; but he is a man suspended in a limbo between action and loss of will. A decision – more important than the act of leaving the Villa for the Castello – is at work in him. Secretly, while he has lain purblind, indulged and pleasantly adrift in the Imperial bed, something he cannot identify has happened to William, is still happening.

And in rather the same way the Castello comes to life again, warily. Felix pokes his head outside his burrow and blinks at the midday sun. His nose twitches. The garbage smell the rain had drawn from the earth lingers faintly but overlaid with more pleasant scents, heady, not all familiar. He nods good-day at the Misses Head and Stimpson who are climbing the path to the upper gardens, heads bobbing to one side then the other as they identify new growths the soil had been harbouring secretly and has now thrust forth to meet the sun. Miss Head pronounces, Miss Stimpson lollops behind, pausing to make notes on a small pad. 'I say, Cissie, hold on.' She thrusts the pad in the pocket of her cloak and takes the steps three at a time with the bounding gait of an ungainly schoolgirl.

Shall I go out? wonders Felix. The weather is better, his oppression is lifting, though the humidity makes him breathless. Someone is playing a cello, its beautiful deep-throated sobs are joined by higher-voiced strings and a first hesitant then fluent piano. A concert must be in preparation. A theme is stated and then before the message can be delivered, restated. A workman passes Felix's door carrying bucket, pasting brush and rolls of paper. He stops about fifty yards away and pastes a poster to the wall. Without his spectacles Felix cannot read it. Undecipherable message.

Normality is returning but the Castello is making an invalid's recovery. There is a feeling that life is not yet exactly as it was. Something has happened.

The Japanese minibus has arrived to pursue Dante but a crowd has gathered in reception. The ten o'clock coach to Florence did not leave. Will the coach go to Florence? Will the newspapers come from Florence? Everyone has different information. Ferdinando, besieged, raises one hand to hold the enquirers at bay and to beseech silence and with the other grasps the telephone. He speaks. He listens. He shouts. He shakes the receiver as if to empty it of water. He cradles the receiver between his head and shoulder, freeing his hand to cover his ear. He thinks of giving in his notice and how peaceful it would be without these foreigners always wanting information, but he would miss too much the dignity of his post behind the important desk in the handsome gatehouse (besides he is saving to buy an Alfetta, a motor-boat and video-cassette recorder, or perhaps to go to America).

Defeated, Ferdinando holds out the receiver as though to demonstrate that he is helpless, the connection with Florence is still not fully restored, the coach is in the car-park of the Castello but where is the driver?

'No information today. Tomorrow there will be information.'

The Americans in particular are indignant. Even though (unlike the hordes below in the city) they are quietly dressed, soft-spoken Europhiles, they expect, having paid the high price for their trip, that the machinery of life will not break down. They would be affronted to be treated as tourists, back home on campus they will tell their travellers' tales of European muddle with fond self-deprecating smiles; nevertheless, having brought their cultured heads and soft loo paper all the way to Tuscany, having made allowances, they can claim at least the right to know why things are not working.

Ferdinando sweats. He slams down the telephone. He loses the English so painfully acquired as a Soho waiter, refined by Berlitz. He shrugs. He turns his back on Babel.

Fanny, having dressed, having decided to go out into the sun, rests for a moment on her bed and falls asleep. Her dream is strange and rather beautiful, though not one she could interpret on waking. She stands in a garden. An unseen hand offers her a single lily and a single rose. The garden is in sunlight but the sky is black. She smiles with surprise as she sees that the sun, the moon and a single star all hang in the sky at once.

Between dream and waking she feels unusually peaceful and at the same time surprised: as if she had been both blessed and summoned. Someone is calling her. She is called from sleep by a soft voice.

'Signora?'

'Maria! I'm sorry. Mi scusi.'

Is this Maria of the Smiles or Tears? Fanny wakes to find the chambermaid of the blown-up brother-in-law standing by her bed. At first it seems a miracle that the woman she left grieving should have made her way (presumably) from a sorrowing family in Pisa to Fanny's bedside. But then it is not so odd. The rain has stopped. The sun has come out. Operatic chambermaids must return to their work.

But this is not a story, it is life (and death) and Fanny wishes fervently at this moment that there were a common language in which she could offer at least the words of consolation and welcome: I am sorry.

Instead it is Maria who is holding out to Fanny first the handkerchief Fanny left in her hands the day Maria wept and everyone went to Florence. It has been washed and ironed. Fanny shakes her head, no, and in place of the handkerchief Maria is beamingly proffering a bunch of roses as red as you might find in an English garden. Beaming and nodding.

Fanny takes them. They have no scent but they are fresh and so abundant they spill from her hands on to the bedspread.

Fanny laughs. So does Maria. But who?

'Che?'

'Buon uomo.'

What good man? Maria shakes her head and points out the postcard that comes with the roses. She opens the door of Bronzino and points to the step. The roses have been found on the step. Maria is positively skittish. The roses have put her in the mood for opera buffa in which mysterious suitors place roses on doorsteps and leave without so much as an aria. She wants a drama, a conspiracy, a delicious confusion and Fanny cannot bring herself to disappoint her although she guesses the roses must be from William. Who else?

She indicates thank you and no, Maria must not think of cleaning Bronzino. She picks up the postcard. No message.

'L'Annunziazione,' says Maria, points to her belly, crosses herself and exits with mop and bucket.

When Maria has left Fanny gets up slowly. She finds the handkerchief on the dresser and wishes Maria had kept it. She puts the roses in a jug of water, thinking of Willy. Glancing out of the window she sees Lisa signalling: come out. She waves back, I'm coming. Just as she is about to open the door she finds the card fallen to the floor and recognises it as the Annunciation she had liked best in the Uffizi. Melozzo da Forli: Gabriel a boy delivering a message, the Virgin a real girl, taken unawares. Fanny slips the card with the handkerchief into the drawer where she keeps her growing collection of annunciations. On second thoughts, she takes back the Forli and puts it in her handbag, then she goes out to join Lisa.

They sit in one of the high-hedged gardens, faces raised to the sun. Fanny feels not unpleasantly strange, both weak and peaceful, the sun working in her, her mind almost still, her breasts heavy.

'I had such a funny dream. Rather nice.'

Signals. Messages. Misunderstandings.

There is great indignation. While Ferdinando had been struggling with the telephone and furious foreigners, the coach for Florence departed unnoticed, empty. It is not the driver's business whether or not his coach is empty or full. No one had told him not to go to Florence so down the hill he sways, enjoying his own air-conditioning and opera turned up full on the radio. He sings along with Rossini, Verdi, Puccini, and when a newsflash interrupts he continues to sing, so missing the latest information on the hijacked plane. He sings for the photograph of his wife and children hung above the dashboard with a plastic rose and a crucifix. He sings for the happy wife, the smiling children, the dying Christ. He sings for the sunshine. O sole mio!

*   *   *

William tries to telephone the Castello from the Villa Inglese to say that now the road is clear Daisy's Leonardo will be driving him back in the Audi but when Ferdinando flung down the receiver this morning he left it off the hook so no connection can be made.

Dozing in the shade Fanny imagines the strength returning to her limbs. She wonders why she does not tell Lisa about the red roses or about Perdita. It is not exactly that she is keeping secrets but as she rests in her not unpleasant invalidism, the mood of the beautiful dream is still with her. It has in some way emptied her mind of everything else. Looking up at the pattern of leaves, observing through half-closed lids Lisa's abundant downy flesh still worshipping the sun, the head and shoulders of a workman on the other side of the hedge carrying a ladder over one shoulder and a big brush in a bucket suspended from the other, Fanny imagines her skull as a delicate porcelain vessel through which a golden light dimly glows. William, Alison, Rob, Perdita, Maria, Sebastian – the faces which had so urgently presented themselves earlier today, troubling her, calling – recede, retreat along with all other matters of the world of action, concern, revelation. It is years (she cannot remember when) since Fanny has felt so luxuriously irresponsible. Has she earned the right to such rest? Even that question is as wafer-light as the leaf that falls, spiralling with infinite slowness, into her lap, or the vapour-trails of other, dashing lives in the sky above.

And now here in Michelangelo at dusk is Jay's gentle moon-face offering a most delicious convalescent's picnic which, being Jay, he has conjured out of the thin air. Another prawn? A little mayonnaise? Nectarine washed in Perrier? He is not at all certain she should be up.

'But I'm lying down.'

'Are you sure you're all right?'

'Fine. There must be something in those pills. Really, Jay.'

They are all floating, Jay and Fanny and Lisa, suspended in this high, calm room above earthly troubles. Quite the best room in the Castello. Lucky Jay. 'Aren't we lucky?' Below, the concert is in progress. Cello, strings and piano have finally come together and Mozart makes sense of everything.

From the dark tower lights flash in a pattern that appears to be regular. Signals? A camp-fire flowers in the site outside the walls. As Fanny takes the few steps home across the terrace from Michelangelo to humbler Bronzino, before she sees the thin violet shadow across her bed hunched around a smaller shape no bigger than a parcel, she is caught for a moment in the now sharper night air by the wonder of a falling star and then another and another, the river of lights below signalling mankind at home in peace. And Mozart uttering a final chord that states: this is the world, it has such a harmony. Listen!

NINE

'Perdita?'

Fanny turns on the light, startling the girl, who had been sleeping. For a second she seems unsure where she is then she stands shakily, leaving the baby curled on the bed. He sleeps placidly with half his fist in his mouth. Perdita looks even thinner, sick and exhausted.

'Mrs Farmer. I'm ever so sorry but I didn't know what to do. I came and they said you were very ill. Are you ill? We can go away.'

'I'm fine. Perdita, please sit down. Don't talk.' Fanny, normally so competent, is almost as startled as Perdita. This is a miracle. It is also a shock to be shaken so abruptly from her delicious drifting mood. Food, she thinks, drink. 'I'm afraid I've only got biscuits and fruit. But I can make you some coffee on the ring. Unless you'd rather have juice? There's a little fridge.' Fanny is behaving like a housewife. 'There might be some milk. Does Mario drink milk?'

'That's all right. I'm feeding him myself. I mean, I tried to start weaning him but it was difficult. I didn't know what to get. He didn't like the powdered stuff from the shop, then there weren't any shops.'

Irrelevantly, Fanny wonders that such a starveling could have any milk in her. Her hand shakes as she pours the water on the coffee, arranges the biscuits on a plate, a nectarine (the last and overripe) on a glass saucer, finds the tray and moves the narrow coffee table to the bed. No sugar. She looks as if she could do with sugar. No sugar worth speaking of in those boring Italian biscuits.

'I'm sorry the biscuits are boring.'

Perdita, nibbling, looks at Fanny as if she were speaking a foreign language. She takes tiny bites of biscuit and minute sips of coffee. Fanny perches at the end of the narrow sofa but finds it hard to sit still. She gets up and turns on the bedside lamp, switches off the harsh overhead light. She wishes she could have a drink but antibiotics and alcohol don't mix, do they? If they were antibiotics. She makes up her mind and pours Perdita a small brandy, an even smaller one for herself.

'I should drink that slowly.' Perdita seems nervous of both the food and the drink, although she accepts everything, tasting the brandy as if it were medicine, but it does at least bring a little colour to her cheeks. Fanny thinks, she is like a small grain-eating bird in winter, starving but windy of the food table. Her legs are either very brown or very dirty. Time for that later if she doesn't fly away first. And if she doesn't fly away, what am I to do with her? What was I planning when I so frantically pursued her? 'There, that's better.' Fanny clears the tray away and settles again on the end of the sofa. She swallows half her own brandy and surveys the girl, her patch-work skirt torn, her hair tangled, sitting very still like a child waiting to be told off, or told what to do next, or to be sent to bed. In what strange guise, thinks Fanny, does life come charging in.

'I came to look for you, you know.'

Perdita's eyes widen. 'To look for me? Why?'

'I was worried. I got your message but I couldn't understand it. When you phoned.'

'Oh yes, I shouldn't have done that.'

'Of course you should. So I was worried and I went to Florence to find you and Mario. And all the time you were coming up. They said you had gone to the Ospedale, the hospital. I thought you must be ill, or Mario.' Fanny speaks gently and slowly, as if to a foreigner. Don't push. Don't press. 'Are you sure you wouldn't like to have a rest? Sleep?'

'Oh no, I had a lovely sleep, really. You needn't have gone. I wasn't ill. Mario was all right.' All the same Perdita's eyes fill with tears in the most remarkable way. She does not sob, the tears do not fall, she does not wipe her eyes or change her expression but simply says: 'Do you think I could have some more of this? It's nice.' She will tell me now, Fanny thinks, as she takes the glass to pour a second, smaller brandy. But when she turns round the girl has fallen asleep again where she sits, does not stir even when Fanny puts a pillow under her head, covers her legs with a spare blanket from the closet (there is a nip in the air now at night), checks the baby too is sleeping and safe, and switches off the light.

Some time, about four in the morning, Fanny wakes cramped from her doze on the sofa. The bedside light is on again and Perdita has just finished feeding the baby. Her small breasts are still bare and it is hard to believe they ever held nourishment for any infant, but Mario is more than content, crowing and waving sleepy hands, bubbling and subsiding against his mother's shoulder. Groggily, imagining herself for a moment in a dream, Fanny remembers William reading Forster and smiling at the Bellini baby in Caroline Abbott's lap. In the golden loom of the lamp the reality of Perdita and Mario is a little different – the baby fits but the mother not at all.

'Oh, I'm sorry. I didn't mean to wake you. And this is your bed, isn't it.'

'No, please, stay there.'

It is the time of night, the time of death and confidences. Or Perdita finds it easier talking like this. She can hardly see Fanny. She does not cover her breasts. She speaks first awkwardly as if words are hard to find.

'I took him to that hospital place with the babies on the wall. I asked. Someone told me, they still take babies, it's a very old place for that. I thought it was a museum.'

Fanny whispers: 'The Spedale degli Innocenti.'

'I don't know. But I was really going to leave him. It was awful. It was raining, it was silly, I kept thinking he mustn't get wet. But you see his granny wouldn't have us any more, after they said it was Sergio in that plane, and the police came. When I saw you in those gardens the old cow had said we'd got to go but I didn't think she wouldn't want Mario. That's what Sergio had said. I was to bring the baby and his mother would be there and he'd come back. Then we'd see what to do. I thought they

were nice to babies here. She kept screaming at me in Italian
and I didn't understand. D'you know Italian?'

'No.'

'It sounds nice, like music, but it doesn't mean anything unless
you know it, does it?'

'Perdita, what about your family? Won't they help?'

'They don't want to know, do they. Then the old cow told me
about this hospital place.'

'And why didn't you leave him? In the end?'

'I couldn't. I don't know why. I didn't think I liked babies. But
he's nice, isn't he?'

'He's lovely.' Fanny has pulled on her wrap. Now it is Perdita
who sounds so heart-breakingly matter-of-fact in her dull little
voice, Fanny who is close to tears as they look down at Mario.
She turns to the girl. 'Oh my dear, my poor dear.'

Mario grunts, his mouth turned down. He has gone red in the
face. Fanny remembers. 'I think he needs changing.'

'Yes. I got some of those things you can throw away but
they're too expensive. I don't know what I'll do when they're
gone.'

'We'll see in the morning. Let's both get some sleep.'

Mario changed, his mother asleep, all is well in Bronzino,
except that Fanny cannot get to sleep again. She has committed
an act of unreason but for the moment at least that does
not concern her. Instead, beneath her closed lids images flit:
Sebastian's imagined face, the della Robbia foundlings, Forli's
Virgin and Botticelli's pagan Spring, the wonderful dream of the
lily, the rose, the sun, moon and star. There are connections it
seems to Fanny, but she cannot grasp them, she is falling asleep.
Words come to her but they might be in a foreign tongue for all
they mean. Annunciation. Something lost. Something found.

'Now I've found you I don't want to lose you.'

Daisy is desolate at the thought of William's departure. Sometimes it entirely slips her mind how he came to be there. When
she does remember she supposes that skinny what's-her-name
wife with the frizzy hair (you'd think she'd get it straightened)
will want him back but Daisy has the ruthlessness of the utterly

lonely. Little Mrs Thing will have plenty of people, one does at that age, lots of fun, everyone wanting to be with you, Daisy remembers. Tottering on William's arm in the lower garden, she would kidnap him if she could. As it is she tries to hold him with the fragile threads of their short intimacy. For they are friends, she is sure of that. And why not? Age speaking with age is the dullest of conversations. The girl who so wistfully survives within the cage of Daisy's brittle bones responds to William's gallantry with something like flirtation.

'You don't think this scarf is too bright? The green, I mean.'

William, though abstracted, really looks. Daisy moves him.

'Not at all. The brighter the better.'

'Oh pish, I know what you think. Silly old Dodo dressed to kill. Potty never noticed. Could have worn a hamster on my head, he'd never see.' Daisy makes an excuse to pause. The truth is, she is breathless but anxious not to hang too heavily on William's arm. 'Look, that poor little rose still flowering. Can't think how it's survived. Leonardo pulls up the flowers and waters the weeds.' Still hanging on his arm but stooping, she snaps off the thin rose head and gives it to William. 'You'd never believe it now but this is the English garden.'

'English?'

'Present from Potty. I'd had an accident. Lost a baby. Potty carried me down here blindfolded, if you can credit it, one evening after rain. I could smell it before I saw it: honeysuckle, roses and that great big lily with the golden middle you get a yellow nose if you sniff. What's it called? Madonna?'

'My wife lost a baby.'

'Pelvis too narrow, I expect. Pouff! We could sit for just a minute. You can get the scent sometimes still. No, hold my hand, I like that.'

'Did you mind? The baby?'

'Mind? Mind? Oh, I expect one minded everything then. Such a fuss.'

Has she dropped off again? Where is she? Back in some Tuscan evening, her eyes closed as she catches the ghosts of sweet cottage scents? No. Daisy is still here. The minutest pressure on William's hand, almost a squeeze. And then she lets

him go and William looks around in vague amazement, nearly
wonder, detecting the buried garden beneath the wilderness of
bramble and convolvulus. He thinks of phlox, lupin, delphinium,
lavender, verbena, the quince outside his own study window,
and wonders what it was like to live like this in exile. He believes
he knows. He has lived like this himself without leaving home.
Quite suddenly, as though he had been summoned, he wants to
be back with Fanny. He can puzzle no further yet but the urge
to go is so strong his body must have tensed, for Daisy senses
it.

'You're off, aren't you?'

'I think I should go.'

'Then I'll have to let you. Go on. Off with you.'

'I don't know how to thank you.' William stands awkwardly
but Daisy gives him an actual physical push. 'Can't I help you
back to the house? It's quite a climb.'

A glint of the green eye. There is a conspiracy of loss between
them.

'Stop here a bit. Daisy'll stay.' From time to time William
suspects that this is another of Daisy's games, parodying her
own decay.

'Well then.' William turns to start the climb up to the house.

'We had fun, didn't we? Eh?'

'We did.'

He goes on up and in her garden she sits, sighs, snorts at her
own folly and hums to some secret music in her head. Who's to
hear? Daisy all alone-oh.

While William in the Audi (Leonardo not to be found, drinking
Daisy's wine in the garden shed) begins the ascent from the
Villa Inglese to San Salvatore (at least the tank has been filled),
sucking his thumb because he has pricked it on Daisy's rose,
those abroad in the Castello remark on the excellence of last
night's concert, the arrival of the newspapers, the coaches
running on time again, the air as clear as if it had been washed,
the golden light streaming from the middle air that signals the
end of summer, the winter they will not be here to witness; and
particularly there is interest in the posters advertising most

colourfully the Festa della Santa Maria del Castello, San Salvatore, 29 settembre. What could possibly be wrong with a world which on such a splendid day promises a festa?

'A festa then?' William, having left the Villa Inglese, made up his mind, is in good spirits and impatient to see Fanny. Already he is imagining their reunion as he parks the car and walks by the gatehouse into the Castello. He joins Miss Head and Miss Stimpson surveying the poster which depicts an unusual Madonna – rather cheap-looking and weeping what appear to be tears of blood.

Miss Head turns. 'Hello, Mr Farmer. You're better then. Oh yes. Always fun. Nothing like Siena, of course, but there's always a good turn-out, isn't there, Win. Win doesn't like the fireworks.'

'No, not frightfully.' Miss Stimpson blushes and ducks her head under the resurrected floppy sunhat. 'At home I used to go in the cupboard with the dogs. I say, Mr Farmer, you're bleeding.'

'Only a rose.' William sucks his thumb absently. He still holds Daisy's rose and is in a hurry to deliver it to Fanny. 'Excuse me.'

Others are gathering around the poster. The little Dutch couple are holding hands and smiling. Even the film director is smiling benevolently upon his nymphs. The idea of a festa seems to have made everyone nicer. As William leaves, Miss Head is explaining to the Dutch couple very slowly in case they do not understand that the festa is a fine example of the joining of pagan and Christian elements, superstition and religion. The Dutch peg-people nod and smile; they are kind and polite and do not wish to hurt Miss Head's feelings by explaining that Mrs Peg is a Professor of English and Mr Peg an Authority on Religion and Superstitions of the Western Mediterranean.

When Mr and Mrs Peg have smiled thank-you and goodbye Miss Stimpson and Miss Head continue their walk up the hill. Miss Stimpson seems to be plucking up courage to say something.

'Cissie, we have been friends for a long time.'

'Yes?'

'I think that sometimes you explain things too much.' Having spoken she goes further. 'People do not always want things explained.'

Miss Head is startled. This is not like Win at all. This is the second time lately Win has behaved in a way not like herself. Can she have changed? Can one change? Where has the biddable Win found such courage? She might just as well have sprouted wings.

Lost and found.

In Fra Angelico Felix is later than usual getting started because he was reading very late last night. Uncharacteristically, his mind has wandered. This has happened more than once since he came to the Castello. He has not exactly lost his taste for research but finds himself, in the strict reading programme he had laid down, increasingly beguiled by red herrings. First Christianity. Then, last night, having reached the Annunciation, Gabriel reminded him of something almost forgotten and he turned back to the book of Daniel and thence to Genesis and Enoch. As he read, he must have fallen asleep for he woke, cramped, as though he had dreamed, to a most unscholarly apprehension of angelology. Or rather he imagined (for what could it be but imagination?) that a cloud of angels had gathered in his small cell and were hushing him asleep; and in his sleep he had a dream (unbecoming as he saw it to his age and status) that Ada was twenty and they were making love in the most explicit and precisely recollected detail. About a year after their marriage when each knew what pleased the other and Ada teased and laughed in the room at the Villa Inglese, then he demanded and groaned and she began wonderfully to sing.

Felix woke still dressed on the crumpled bedcover in the absolute certainty that Ada still lived, the angels had told him. It took him more than a couple of hours to change his clothes, shave his widower's face and to grasp that Ada was not here and would never be here again, in this life. He cut himself shaving, stuck on a piece of tissue, drank a cup of coffee, sat until he had stilled himself from trembling.

Now he emerges in a state of mind between joy and loss, wipes his spectacles and in the bright golden morning studies the poster he had not been able to decipher the day before.

Festa. Well. That at least is a clear message.

William is climbing the hill to Bronzino. He wraps a handkerchief round the rose and holds it still. He climbs like a lover. He imagines the reunion with Fanny. He has held too much back. He has never told her enough how much he loves her. He is climbing for his life.

Lisa walks into Bronzino without knocking. She has been awake half the night, telling herself that at her age there is nothing at all to worry about but she needs someone else to tell her not to worry and Fanny is the only possible person. She notes that it is a beautiful morning. Lisa's spirit, on holiday, inclines to optimism. Whatever could be wrong on such a day?

'My God, Fan. What's that?'

'A baby.'

'I can see that. But what are you doing with it?'

'Well. Do you remember Perdita, the girl on the bus from Pisa?' Fanny explains. While Perdita takes a long shower Fanny has been busy emptying one of the large dresser drawers and lining it to make a cot. 'There, d'you think that will be all right?'

Lisa flops on to the bed next to Mario.

'So that's what you were up to in Florence. Fan, you're insane. But he is rather sweet, isn't he. Whatever will Willy say?'

'What will Willy say about what?'

Enter William the ardent lover, panting, the rose clutched in his handkerchief. He takes in the scene, disappointed not to find Fanny alone. But what is Fanny doing? Why is Lisa laughing?

'Willy, darling!'

'Hello, Lisa. Fanny, darling.'

'Are you better?'

'My God, Fan. What's that?'

'A baby.'

'I can see that. But where did you get it?'

Fanny looks pale, thin, as if she had been ill. But she has a triumphant and slightly dangerous air.

'You could say I found him. Or he found me.'

William gapes. He sinks into Bronzino's one chair. He opens his mouth.

Clang of a bucket off stage and enter Maria of the Smiles.

'Buon giorno, signora. Ma cos'è questo! Un bambino!' The bucket is dropped and Mario (della Robbia founding no more but Bellini cherub) is gathered up in the arms of Maria. It is a touching and beautiful scene.

Some Italians still love babies, after all.

Only after Lisa has gone to tell Jay and Fanny and Maria are engaged, busy clucking in admiration of the miraculous infant (his smile, his fingers, his eyes, his toes, his tuft of black hair, his warm olive skin, his mere existence here in this room), does William realise that he is still clutching Daisy's rose.

But what is this on the table in the jug?

Where did they come from, all the red roses?

The lovely day, the kind of day advertised on the brochure for San Salvatore – sky postcard blue, cypress eternally green, little oaks crisply gilded – has become a very complicated day.

At the centre of it all is Perdita, passive and cleaner. Does she have an opinion? For a while no one thinks of asking her, so concerned are they for her predicament. Ferdinando with distaste and an indifference amounting almost to an opinion has astonishingly produced disposable nappies from the small store for the convenience of guests of the Castello where there are facilities for playing children but nuclear families are actually hardly ever seen.

He is in any case totally and importantly occupied by the preparations for the Festa. These are gradually taking over the Castello as an overheated lorry sits fainting in the car-park, delivered of workmen with ladders, fairy lights, equipment for son et lumière, banners, bunting, lamps and microphones. It becomes almost impossible to circulate in the narrow streets and the difficult path leading up to the chapel of Santa Maria del

Castello is chiuso, absolutely closed to anyone mad enough to want to ascend it in the midday sun. The workmen do not want to ascend it. They sit beneath the laurels yawning and complaining. Ferdinando has become a vespa. He closes reception and buzzes around shouting and threatening and cajoling but no one observes him. He has no sting.

'Shoo.' Fanny bats at a wasp but what's the point? They are drunk on fruit suddenly overripe to bursting from the hot sun after so much rain. Sitting on the terrace that joins Michelangelo to Bronzino, Fanny supposes it must be the antibiotics and the bad night. She feels dreamy, pleasantly distanced from the need to make a decision. Perdita sits a little back from the rest, cross-legged on the ground. Jay, of all people, appears fascinated by Mario. He bends over the cot-drawer, waves his fingers, makes un Jay-like noises. 'D'you think it would be all right if I picked him up?'

Lisa is being sensible. Lisa can be dauntingly sensible.

'Well, they can't stay here, can they?'

Miss Stimpson and Miss Head pass below the wall and wave. Don't be silly Win, it couldn't be a baby.

'So what do we do?' William is speaking to Lisa but watching Fanny.

Jay will not have them sent back to Florence. He shudders. His remembrance of Florence is not happy.

William doesn't know.

Fanny shakes her head.

'The camp,' says Lisa. 'For the moment. While we decide.'

'Is it clean?' Fanny worries.

'Then we get on to the British consulate or whatever.'

Fanny nods. Decisions seem as powerless as the tumbling bumble-bee on the geranium. The impotence of action.

'Look. There's Felix. He hasn't got his hat on.'

'Felix, you haven't got your hat on!' Fanny shouts and points to her head.

It takes a moment for Felix to receive the signal. He is still trying to interpret the message of his dream. Ah, yes. His hat. He waves thank-you. They seem to be having a party up there.

'Hold on,' says Lisa, nips back to Michelangelo and returns with a litre bottle of white wine and plastic mugs. The bottle is chilled, so green, so cool. What a good idea.

In spite of the antibiotics Fanny drinks. In spite of his tummy so does Jay. He too has found something: a quiet determination to enjoy himself. Lisa opens her mouth to demur and closes it. Something has happened to Jay and she is not quite sure if she likes it or not.

'Jay, if you want a drink you'll have to put the baby down.'

'I don't see why.'

So he drinks, a benign Bacchus, one arm for Mario contented on his lap, the other for his glass.

Lisa stands. They smile up at her. In her opinion they are behaving like children.

'So what have we decided?'

It is William who drains his glass first and startles them all.

'I think we should ask Perdita. What do you want to do, Perdita?'

At that moment Fanny loves him. She looks at this husband who can still surprise her as though to say: oh, there you are. He has taken Perdita's hand and led her to a chair. He sits down facing her and gently repeats his question. Perdita is clean now, she has even washed her skirt and put it on again straightaway. It gives her the appearance of an orphaned mermaid risen from the sea to ask the way. Her fate is being decided yet her face is still empty, unwritten-on. She speaks so softly they can hardly hear, with the effort of someone roused from a dream.

'I don't mind really. You've all been very kind.'

William presses but not enough to alarm her.

'Are you happy to go to the camp?'

'Oh yes.'

'And then what do you want to do? You see, we won't be here much longer. We can't leave you like this.'

Her smile really is very beautiful.

'Sergio will come. I'll wait for him. I left a message with a friend of his.' She addresses Fanny. 'The one who gave me the lift that day we met in Fiesole. He couldn't help but he could take the message. I think I'd better feed Mario now.'

When Perdita has gone inside Lisa wants to know: 'Who's Sergio?'

Fanny sighs. 'Sergio Dolci. It was on the news. That terrorist in the plane. Of course, even if he survives he can't possibly come.'

'Oh, Lord. Fanny, you and your lame dogs.'

'It's the baby I'm worried about.'

They are concerned. They are all decent concerned people who cannot make up their minds. They have another drink. A second van – it looks like a caterer's – has drawn up in the car-park. In the little central square Ferdinando is shouting at someone. The responsibility of the Festa is too much. How, without a bonus, can he alone make everything work? He waves his arms, he groans. Povero Ferdinando! Dio mio! What an opera!

'Fan, you must lie down. You've been ill. And I didn't know.'

'So have you.'

Willy finishes shaving himself. He peers in the mirror. The hornet has left a tiny livid mark that may never go away. Otherwise William is better.

'That was an accident.'

'A siesta would be nice.'

They lie side by side on the letto matrimonale. Outside the world burns up. Perdita lies on her side in the airy green tent. It is clean and comfortable and paid for. The other campers are very nice although most of them speak languages she does not know. Lisa has driven to Fiesole and come back with feeding bottles, sterilising liquid and a formula Mario has accepted. Perdita bends over her baby. She wants to cuddle him but he is asleep. She whispers: 'You will understand, won't you. Please. I know you will.'

Fanny feels she must explain so that William can understand.

'So you see it was the right place all that time – the Ospedale, I mean. Perdita had been there and I missed her. Then she came here and there was a muddle. I was ill.'

'Shush.' William takes her hand. He wants to make love to

her, not from simple passion but in a way that is somehow connected with his wonderings as he lay purblind in the Villa Inglese. As though he wanted to tell her something he cannot express. But although she lies still and has no temperature there is something feverish about Fanny.

'When I went to Florence, after I'd seen you at the Villa, I think I was a bit mad. Perhaps I was ill already.' Fanny turns her head. With her free hand she touches William's cheek, the bright mark of the hornet. 'But what about you? Did you get your Forster stuff from that funny Mrs Pottinger?'

'I think I might leave that.'

'The monograph? Willy! But you've been on it for years! Did something happen at the Villa!'

'Nothing I can explain. Nothing that matters.'

They close their eyes but neither sleeps. William says: 'You want to keep it, don't you? The baby?'

'Oh, Willy! How can we?' Her face is flushed, smiling, her eyes too bright. 'Could we?'

He kisses her eyes, her mouth, her throat, her breasts. They make love and there is nothing extraordinary about that yet they are both surprised, as if something wonderful had happened.

William whispers: 'I forgot to tell you. I brought you a rose.'

'But you sent me those lovely roses. I forgot to say. And the Annunciation.'

'What roses?'

'Buona sera, San Salvatore!'

Speaking from the sky the voice of God announcing the Apocalypse shakes the Castello rudely from its siesta. Fanny and William jump. Lisa, lying on her stomach, groans and covers her ears. Jay, eyes still closed, reaches automatically for the telephone. Felix rubs his eyes. 'Ada?'

It is Ferdinando proudly testing the public address system installed for the Festa. For the first time today he is pleased. Heads appear from windows, campers from tents, all the film director's Jackanory girls run out naked on to the terrace, squealing. Ock? says Mr Peg the Dutchman.

No one goes to sleep again. They have all slept too long

anyway, it is almost evening. It might have been a spell. They could have been enchanted. In fact, as they stagger out groggily and look up they understand: the golden day has melted to be replaced by a low white sky. Also, something else has happened. Rumour is abuzz again along with the fat flies that fall into the six o'clock drink. The workmen have awoken and the preparations for the Festa proceed, causing nuisance everywhere. But subjects of the most interested speculation are two black official-looking cars (police?) that have arrived while everyone slept, and ignoring the car-park dashed to a halt just inside the gatehouse. And now, as they watch and wonder, a giant bluebottle of a helicopter is first heard and then seen hovering and finally lowering itself on to the pad, dwarfing the Marchese's little yellow machine.

Lisa calls out from the bar. 'Nando, what's happening?'

Nando, having consumed the best part of a bottle of vodka (donated in the spring by a grateful American matron), might have been able to tell them what is happening but his brief triumph with the public address system over, is not interested in telling anybody anything. He shrugs, raises his hands to the sky and walks on down, acquainted with more sorrows than anyone – including his mother, his fiancée in Fiesole and his mistress in Pisa – could possibly understand. How can he bear this burden? In America it would be different. Everything would be different in America.

Time for dinner. The men lead the way. Fanny falls behind with Lisa.

'Lisa? Have you given up your Italian lessons?'

'Lost my diaphragm, haven't I?'

'Diaphragm?'

'You know, Dutch cap. What we all had before the pill sent us off our heads. Didn't think it mattered any more.'

'Oh, Lisa, I'm sorry. I'm sure it doesn't. You're not worried?'

Lisa grins. 'Of course not. You know me, Fan. I don't worry.' Lisa stomps on. Fanny finds it hard to imagine anything in the world that could defeat Lisa. Must be the weather. Hard to breathe. Lisa's always susceptible to weather.

What's going on? A German Professor of Italian with a radio

says investigations are being strenuously pursued in connection with the Vatican bomb plot. Fabrizio has laboured all day – or so he would have it seem – to produce his masterpiece: la regina dei funghi. Twitters of excitement from his favoured clients. A mushroom is a mushroom says Lisa and pushes away her plate. Felix has borrowed a newspaper from Mr and Mrs Peg. Unfortunately it is in Dutch but he labours with the headlines. America has invaded somewhere or other, again. Or else America has been invaded? That doesn't seem very likely. Someone has heard something about the Marchese. Does anyone know anything about the Marchese? Fabrizio's mushrooms smell peculiar as if they had been dwelling in some unspeakably dark corner of the forest. Lisa's right. Let's have an omelette. Look, here's a copy of yesterday's *Figaro*! Third page, small paragraph: Le hijack est terminé. Please, says Fanny, let me see. Sergio Dolci believed to be dead. On croit but one does not know. Dolci has no known connections. Le hijack of the British airliner apparently without purpose. Terminated. Fanny, love, why are you crying? I don't know. I don't know.

Lisa has lost her diaphragm. Daisy has lost William. Felix tricked by a dream half-believes he has found Ada. Win Stimpson has found courage. Perdita has almost certainly lost Sergio. Fanny has found a baby.

They stand in the dusk on the terrace of Bronzino with their small joys and troubles while in the Castello some other drama, larger and more dangerous than their own story, seems to be taking place, as every light in the tower blazes, yet another black helicopter lands, there are figures on the hill above the camp, and the public address system crackles. Or it might be thunder. The Castello is suddenly at the centre of a web of dangerous action, the world has broken through the walls.

Miss Stimpson and Miss Head pass below on their way back to Giotto from their evening constitutional.

'Will it be fine for the Festa?'

Oh yes, surely, it must be fine for the Festa.

TEN

In Italy it does not rain in September. The sun shines, the olive ripens. Yet last night there was a deluge. Unlike the earlier rains that have punctuated the holiday, this downpour came virtually without warning – no thunder, no lightning – and with such fury that in one night the lower streets of San Salvatore have become streams. And this time Florence has entirely escaped. The field of folk who go hither and thither on the sunny plain below raise their faces from their Blue Guides and point upwards to the hills that waver behind a veil of heaped clouds.

At San Salvatore early risers in the houses and apartments at the bottom of the hill under the walls step from their doors to find themselves paddling. Miss Head goes back for boots. Miss Stimpson kicks off her sandals and laughs like a girl on a beach. Then she remembers the Festa. How awful if the Festa were cancelled!

The sun, already intensely hot between the showers, teases them. They call from window to window, terrace to terrace: What terrible weather! Will the Festa take place?

'Perdita!' Fanny calls to William at the window: 'Is the camp still there? Look through the binoculars.'

'The tents are there but I can't see anyone. I expect they're still asleep. I say, there's Win Stimpson with no shoes on.'

William waves. 'Good morning.'

Miss Stimpson calls back. She comes from reception bearing glad tidings for all: 'It's on! The Festa! Trumpets at six!' She lollops on, a happy messenger, feet if not winged at least bare.

'What's on?'

'The Festa.'

'Oh, the Festa.'

Maria of the Smiles arrives early to be finished in time for the Festa. She runs from casa to casa dodging the rain. She is full of Italian – somehow she has convinced herself that Fanny understands. She runs around Bronzino. She empties the waste-paper basket into a black plastic sack. Pioggia! She mops the floor. Polizia! She looks at the roses, takes the vase to the tap, pours away the water and renews it. She beams at half-dressed Fanny, makes the bed and dusts the desk which is not dusty. Festa? Oh yes, Fanny nods, we are happy for the Festa (are we?). But what about the polizia? Fanny cannot find her phrase-book. La notte? Un incidente? Ah yes! Maria flicks her duster everywhere, over the books, the table, the window-sill, the roses. She clucks and shakes her head. The Marchese. The polizia have taken away the Marchese. Bomba. Il Papa. Then at the window Maria is all smiles again: 'Ecco! La Madonna!'

So it is. Fanny and William, Lisa and Jay, along with most of the guests of the Castello draped in inadequate waterproofs (in Italy it does not rain in September), are huddled in doorways around the little square or in the bar to witness the setting-up of the Madonna, who has been brought down the slippery slope from her chapel at some early hour this morning or perhaps last night. One feels there should be a priest at least to receive her but instead the workmen who yesterday had been sleeping under the laurels are working in the rain. It seems somehow irreverent, the way they are manhandling her, roughly washing her blood-stained cheeks, tacking with hammers into her poor plaster a blue hessian gown, hoisting her on to a kind of palanquin or covered litter (the inner roof blue sky pierced with golden stars) and finally, with shouts and effort, flinging a tarpaulin over all.

The job done, off they go, and those who have observed the scene, tourists and atheists all, are surprised by unease. Struck dumb they are as they disperse or sit over their coffee and drinks, glancing from time to time at the lumpy parcel in the square under the rain.

What had we expected, thinks Fanny: redemption? And looks up to catch Jay's eye. They are sharing the same thought.

'I've seen her before,' Fanny says. 'They shouldn't have brought her down.' She doesn't like to imagine the empty chapel, the unguarded graves. 'Well, Felix, what happens next?'

'Nothing till six o'clock. Then the procession starts.'

'And the trumpets sound?'

The little man's smile is wry. He has cut himself shaving and the scrap of tissue on his chin is spotted with blood.

'Ah yes! The trumpets.' How Ada loved the trumpets. They came over from the Villa Inglese and she danced in the streets like a girl.

Felix seems distracted today, thinks Fanny, and he's cut himself shaving.

'Is it true the police were here last night? They took away the Marchese?'

No one knows for certain, any more than they can positively explain what will happen at the Festa. Ah, Mr and Mrs Peg have the expensive programme which can be purchased at reception. Thank you, how kind. Ock. Oh dear, it's in Dutch.

Mrs Peg who wears her greying hair in Dutch-girl braids around her head, shows Fanny the meaningless words, pointing with her finger. The six o'clock trumpets summon all to the Procession of Santa Maria to her cappella. Supplicators mingle picturesquely with the many visitors who come to witness. (Supplicators? That must have something to do with the notes of intercession in the chapel?) The famous Racing up the Hill and Running of the Medici. And now what can that mean? Mrs Peg's English is after all excellent (how embarrassing: they have been treating her as if she did not understand). But this one is difficult. Ah yes! Artificial fires? Oh yes, of course, the French, feu d'artifice. Mrs Peg is pleased. She claps her hands.

Fanny smiles and thanks. Funny about words, she thinks. In a way nothing exists until it is put into words. Our apprehension of the world, if we do not speak the language, is that of an infant. A little understanding is almost worse: the naming of things yields nothing but the surface picture – a child's painting-book in which happy Italians love babies under a blue sky and a golden sun.

'What's up, Fan?' Lisa is three vermouths high.

'I'm worried about Perdita.'

'Oh, that's all right.' Lisa lights a menthol cigarette. 'The campers spent the night in the playroom. They've gone back to their tents.'

'How do you know?'

'Can't remember.' Lisa pulls a face. 'These things make me sick.' She goes on obstinately smoking her cigarette, with a grimace. The atmosphere in the small bar is increasingly thick. Lisa says: 'Did you know the Virgin birth is actually possible? I mean, we don't need men. We can clone ourselves.'

'No, I didn't.'

'Horrid new world.'

'That hath such creatures in't.'

'Hello, Willy. You woken up?'

Lisa is definitely in a queer mood.

'Will, you're the clever one. D'you believe in magic?'

Willy thinks. 'No.'

'Why?' says Fanny, pulling on her jacket.

'It's that damn doll I got in Fiesole.'

'Doll?'

'That ghastly Madonna. I want to chuck it out. But you can't, can you? Even if it was made in Birmingham.'

'Was it?'

'What?'

'Made in Birmingham?'

Lisa snorts. 'What do you think, wise Jay-bird?'

'It's simple. Give it away.'

'Brilliant! I love you Jay! But who to?'

Fanny laughs. 'Let me have it. I'll get rid of it.'

'Bless you, love. Though I suppose it's locking the stable door.'

'What do you mean?' William is puzzled.

Fanny thinks she knows what Lisa means.

Fanny is fastening her hood. William takes her wrist.

'Where are you going?'

'To the camp. I want to make sure Perdita's all right.'

'No you're not. It's pouring and you've been ill. We'll find her later. Lunch now, then rest.'

Leaving the bar, running through the rain, they cannot avoid the sight of Santa Maria in her tarpaulin wrap. Fanny touches the awkward parcel and thinks of the Virgin mother, blind and weeping in the darkness.

High up in the dripping woods below the chapel of Santa Maria del Castello the girl, wrapped in a groundsheet that is almost as good as a tent, plays with her beautiful baby. Earlier, she heard what sounded like the crashing of animals but then there was shouting and through a tunnel in the trees she had just glimpsed a statue being carried on a sort of stretcher down the path. The baby waves at the rain-drops then sleeps and so at last does the girl. Much later she wakens to find the sun has come out, piercing her dark bivouac with wafers of light that lie on the ground, pure gold. Leaving the baby sleeping she creeps from under the groundsheet. She picks a few blackberries and eats them hungrily, the juice staining her lips. She is neither happy nor unhappy. She feels nothing. Then, as her eyes become accustomed to the ragged light, she spots flowers she cannot name. She picks them, absently, along with some of the prettier leaves, until she has a bouquet. But what to do with a bouquet? Dreamily she plucks her posy to pieces and weaves it into a garland for her hair. There might be enough for a necklace. She has almost forgotten the baby. She stands tranced in the wood with flowers in her hair.

William asks Fanny: 'What's the matter with Lisa?'
   'I think she thinks she's pregnant.'
   'Oh dear.'

As though at siesta time a spell had been laid upon the Castello, everyone sleeps and everyone dreams: wild dreams, weeping dreams, laughing dreams, erotic dreams, dancing dreams, dangerous dreams – all frantic and exceptionally vivid, no sweet dreams here. In Fra Angelico Ada comes again to Felix but it is a mocking semblance of Ada, utterly carnal, peremptory. While Felix sobs in his sleep, his heart racing, at Ada's phantasm, Fanny tosses and mumbles, caught in frenzied dance to which she is commanded; the dancers are birds, they are gods, they are trees, she knows and does not know their faces. To find Sebastian she must break from the dance but cruel wings and claws will not permit.

Lisa bites her lip till it bleeds, giving birth to an ugly doll while dim reproachful shades stand at the head of her dream-bed: the lost children. William is lost. He trudges through a limbo heavy as snow. Fanny is calling but his limbs are caught in something more like mud than snow and all pointers, all directions are either obscured or deceitful.

Cissie Head is trying to find her father in a summer field of deep grass. She sees his tall straight back, striding on, but she cannot catch him. She carries a burden: herself, a child. Above her head, in the English sky the colour of a Ruskin-blue bowl, with puffy clouds, Win Stimpson is flying, spreading the wings of her cape, singing of violets. Jay too is flying and even in sleep sees the joke of it – a whale with wings – low over the Nile delta where he sees his love turned to sand and bids goodbye. Roses fall from the sky.

Sleepers awake! the trumpets cry.

'Fan?'

'It's all right. A dream, Willy. We've been dreaming.'

'A nightmare. It must be the weather.'

'I thought I heard trumpets.' Fanny sits up and looks at the travel-clock, alarmed. 'I didn't mean to sleep so long. I was going to look for Perdita.'

William heaves himself off the bed and goes to the window.

'What can you see?'

'Trumpeters on the battlements. Rather splendid. And there are crowds down there.'

Fanny runs to the basin, splashes her face and pulls on clothes, any clothes (the same flower-sprigged dress, in fact, that she wore to Florence in her pursuit of Perdita – Maria has found it, washed, ironed and hung it in the wardrobe). She snatches a shawl.

'Is it raining?'

'Not at the moment. I think it will.'

'Come on then. Willy, wake up.'

'Fanny. Steady. What's the rush?' William turns to look at her, really look at this woman, his wife, and sees a wild female who has not even bothered to brush her hair. He sees a stranger. He sees a witch.

Fanny in turn takes in this man with the livid mark of the hornet on his cheek. At this moment she knows she has it in her power to break something she had believed infrangible.

'Don't you want to go to the Festa?'

'Do you? I'm not sure.'

Well, stay then, damn you.

'Catch me up then.'

The door of Bronzino slams. Jay opens the door of Michelangelo to see Fanny running down the hill. He opens his mouth to call but she won't hear for the trumpets. The door of Fra Angelico stays shut for the moment. Felix is still struggling from his dream to the call of trumpets. Miss Head locks the door of Giotto while Miss Stimpson takes long strides ahead. 'Oh, come on, Cissie! We'll miss the fun!'

The Marchese has vanished but the Festa will continue. Nothing could stop the Festa. Drums join the trumpets and, looking up, the hordes who have poured from coaches all afternoon while the Castello slept, see the black hawk flag of San Salvatore planted on the battlements between each trumpeter. On the field which had been the camp-site, most of the tents have been struck and horses grazing and waiting are attended by figures dressed in medieval tunics and hose. Similarly dressed, but even more splendid – their garb resembling that of beefeaters – eight guards stand evenly spaced around the parcelled Virgin in the roped-off central square. There is an imperative roll on the unseen drum. Something is going to happen.

What's happening? Fanny is too short, she cannot see. A voice calls from above her head: Mrs Peg. 'Come oop.' Oh thank you. Fanny allows herself to be hauled up to the top step of the casa looking on to the square. It seems that everyone she has seen since she came to Tuscany is here, clogging the streets of the Castello, waving, jostling cameras, calling out. There are the nuns from the minibus, the Americans from St Cecilia, the Danes from the Baptistery, the Germans from the European University, the Japanese from their Dante class, even the police-man from Fiesole (she can see the top of his head, it bears a plaster in the shape of a cross) glum between two fat women. There is Maria the chambermaid in a bright red dress, all smiles now. Some of the young – banished from the camp-site – wear Walkman earphones. A girl, with hair so blonde it is white, reaches to kiss a boy with a beard.

But where is Perdita? There must be twenty coaches in the car-park outside the walls and the press of people still passing in by the gatehouse is an incoming wave, a flood-tide forcing those who have arrived early to take their places at the forefront in the square, hard against the ropes. There could be an accident. On the campo outside the walls where the small army of horse-men wait, pennants have been planted in the grass, a field of flags – black hawk on yellow opposing amicably enough at the moment the fleur-de-lys of the Medici. Oh! There's Jay and is that Lisa? Fanny waves, shouts. Have you seen Perdita? But even if they could have heard, at that moment the film director's Jackanory girls surge into the square cutting a careless dance through the crowd and obscuring Jay's egg-shaped head, just as – in the way of mobs – a message is mysteriously passed and a silence ripples from square to gatehouse, a vibrant expectancy. Short Miss Head might have drowned but Miss Stimpson's long periscope neck waves above all.

Oosh! says Mrs Peg, her finger on her lips and a voice rings out. It could be an angel. It is Nando having his finest hour:

'Ecco! La Madonna! La Santa Maria del Castello! Silenzio per la Madonna!'

The beefeaters step forward. Of course, they are butchers and bakers and pizza-makers but for this one day every year something extraordinary happens. As they step forward to remove the tarpaulin, bend in unison and grunt as they raise the Virgin on the litter, they are invested by time, history and ancient rite with a dignity that is greater than the fancy-dress they wear. A bell rings from somewhere above and a priest with acolytes, descending, chants and blesses, sprinkling palanquin, Virgin, bearers and a small yellow dog who chooses this moment to cross the square with water assumed to be Holy. Also a child – no, two children, a boy and a girl in her best party frock – receive their share of water, as, propelled by blushing mothers, they take small steps forward to place posies on the litter and, standing on tiptoe, just manage to kiss the Virgin's feet.

Two hundred cameras click, the crowd awakens and as the litter moves off, swaying, up the hill, those first posies are followed by a hail of roses. Fanny catches one. It is made of paper. Pretty. She sticks it in her hair. William sees her do it. Only a few yards away, he is calling, but she cannot hear him. She has plunged into the crowd. A shirtless boy (well, what's the point of a shirt? It's going to rain) offers her a bottle and she laughs and takes a deep swig. She catches his shoulder. Have you seen a girl with a baby? He shakes his head. He cannot hear or he does not understand. Either.

William is pressed back into a doorway. A nun has stood on his foot. It is definitely going to rain. The procession disappears round the bend up the hill, nuns following immediately behind the litter and a ragged crowd after. He is joined by the anointed dog, hindquarters shaking. Rabid?

'Jay! Have you seen Fanny?'

'You mean she's alone?'

'I tried to stop her.'

'You go this way. I'll go that.'

'Lisa.' William has lost his bearings. It takes him a minute to grasp that they are standing just inside the bar and Lisa looks as if she had been there some time. 'Are you all right?'

'Tiddley-poo.'

Supplicators mingle picturesquely with the many visitors who come to witness, and it is against this stream of people that Fanny tries to make her way to the gatehouse and thence to the camp-site (Perdita, surely, would never have brought Mario into this mob). Running as in those dreams in which one runs but makes no progress, she is aware that among the ordinary folk, the trippers, the guests of the Castello, locals come up perhaps from Fiesole or further, there is another kind of person: women unsmiling, some dressed in black, men stiff in Sunday best, most carrying flowers, real or plastic. Scusi, she says, as she is jolted against one of these solemn pilgrims, brushing the flowers from his hand. She stoops to gather up the flowers but they have already been trampled and the couple moved on. Sorry. So sorry.

The crowd is not disorderly and later will thin, only a small number accompanying the parents of the lost babies on the long climb following the Madonna up the hill, while the rest wait for livelier scenes. Still it takes Fanny nearly an hour to reach the entrance to the Castello and then the great studded doors are barred against her, closed. How can she reach the camp-site if the gates are closed? Why are they closed? Chiuso. A smiling man wags his finger in her face, points up the hill to where the fun is. Fanny is sobbing. No one should sob at the Festa. Why are the gates closed? Il Castello è chiuso. Ferdinando, I want to get out, why can't I get out? But Nando, with his public address system and music system and walkie-talkie and best red play-shirt, is King of the Castle today; he waves away supplicants.

Fanny does not have enough Italian. Who speaks English? She approaches a halberdier at the gate, yawning against his axe-headed staff. He is listening to football on his radio but he likes to speak English. He would like to go to America. American? No, inglese. Shrug. His sympathy for Fanny. Why are the gates locked? The Castello is absolutely closed. The Castle is full of people. No people can come into the Castle. It will be periculous to have more people in the Castle. But I want to get out! I have to find a bambino! Your baby will be all right in Italy. Do you have the key of the Castle? The halberdier is bored. This English conversation is not interesting. To go out of the Castle one must pray at reception. They won't help me at reception! Shrug. The halberdier replaces his earphones. Fanny is not interesting. Juventus is taking a corner. He does not speak English any more.

*   *   *

In Fra Angelico Felix knows that he dreams but cannot wake. There is strange music: a pagan call to frenzy. His lids flutter, he almost wakes, but a heavy hand is pressed on his rib-cage alarming his heart. In his sleep his heart races. To an awakening or to death?

'San Salvatore! La Corsa del Monte! Saint Salvatore! The Running up the Hill!'

The public address system crackles (thunder?) and the announcement is followed by music so loud the horses on the campo are startled. William, still searching for Fanny in the gardens and the lower woods, recognises the Carmina Burana and, for the third time, bumps into Jay on the same mission at the same crossroads by the laurel that marks the start of the path up the hill. Lisa too, looking rather more distractedly for Fanny, wanders in the woods, until, as dusk falls, the music calls her to the path.

Others are summoned from dancing in the square, drinking, making love in secret gardens. What has happened to the Running of the Medici by floodlight on the campo? The horses are restless but in the pause between the solemn procession of the Virgin and the call to the Race, a cloudburst has knocked out both son et lumière. The horse-soldiers lay down their pikes and calm their fretful mounts. Sodden pennants droop. The Medici will not be routed today.

Still, the rain has stopped now and the young men have seized their torches and are straining to run, jostling and mocking, showing off for the girls who laugh and sway like flowers. A gun (or it might have been a thunderclap) and they are off. Breaking the rules of the rite as they have always done, some of the girls are with them, running almost as fast, beating plates, any tin or iron they can snatch up, playing their Bacchic cymbals, shrieking, laughing, goading their boys to run faster.

The trippers, the tourists, the foreigners, the visitors, including most of the guests of the Castello, are in a way beyond explanation held back. They watch the flaming path of the torches, bobbing and dipping among the darkening trees but the music and the frenzy of the run intimate a mystery, a happening upon which only the lost or the least sensitive would intrude.

In the woods, only a few yards from each other but unaware, with the sudden dusk William and Jay are lost but continue to make their way painfully upwards, the way the torches are going. Fanny, lost too, having paused by the laurel, looking for William, has been snatched up in the chase. There is rough laughter as if centaurs carried her along and so she has no choice but to run with the race. When she stumbles a strong arm reaches out to support her and press her on, there is a feral breath on her face, she is borne between the front-runners.

She enters the darkest wood she remembers from the climb with Felix, then at last there are the stone flags, the handrail, and she is flung half-fainting among the small graves. And by the light of a bonfire she catches just one brief vision of a figure at once wonderful, alarming and familiar – Primavera herself, running barefoot, garlanded, with flowers in her hair.

As she emerges from the wood Lisa blinks at the bonfire, the dancing boys and girls. She rubs her scratched legs and in bending catches sight of something on the ground. A garland of flowers, the worse for wear. Someone else, one of the dancers, has seen it too. He picks it up and drops it over Lisa's head. He's rather handsome and Lisa is rather drunk. Well, why not?

The chapel is blessedly empty and cool and everything as Fanny remembers it, except that it is lit, the Lady of the Postcard has had a wash and brush-up and at her hem are many new messages among the mouse-letters and heaped flowers, some fresh. There is a whiff of incense and myrtle. A small cry. Fanny recognises the doll-Christ reaching woodenly for His mother's breast and only then takes in that the capacious font is not empty. Lying on a raggedy knitted grey blanket, Mario, the golden baby, raises his arms for Fanny and crows with joy.

ELEVEN

The Madonna does not weep really for the babies.

The pagan horde were boys and girls and it was not Primavera nor any magic, but Perdita who laid Mario in the font and disappeared among the dancers, shedding flowers, into the darkness.

And it is not the more nimble William but Jay, gasping from the climb, who comes upon the scene in the chapel: a woman, in a posture that strikes him as eternal and symbolic, sitting on the altar steps at the feet of the Madonna, cradling a child. The spotlight that shines on the Madonna has bestowed upon Fanny a halo, suffusing her pale hair with gold. For a moment Jay, dizzy from the haul up the hill, is dazed by the two Madonnas, and by Fanny's face when she raises it. What he sees is rapture.

'Fanny!'

'Hello, Jay. You didn't walk all the way up, did you? Look what I've found.'

Jay lowers his bulk, half-kneeling on the step, a ponderous Magus.

'It's Mario, isn't it.' Jay smiles, reaches out a finger and the baby grips it. 'I'd no idea they were so strong.'

'Oh yes.'

'Where did you find him?'

'In the font. It's a miracle, isn't it. Don't you think?'

Jay nods. How can he bear to contradict her? She is so happy. And he too. For this small space of time he has all in the world he could wish. He can pretend he has all in the world he could wish.

'We ought to go down.'

'I suppose. Look, you've got a flower in your hair. It's a rose.' Gently he tweaks it out. Only paper. He puts it among the other tributes to the Virgin. Fanny is watching him. She has understood something; or rather, something she knew all along has been revealed to her.

'Jay. You sent me those roses, didn't you? And the Annunciation.'

'Yes.'

'Oh, my dear.'

So they go down the black hill, the awkward big man supporting with his arm the woman and the child, leaving behind the dancers, the torches, the bonfire, the graveyard of the babies and the blind Madonna with her painted tears. As they reach the laurel that marks the end of the path the rain comes with no warning – no thunder, no first heavy drops. No god speaking, simply the sky opening, dousing the fire above, below, sending the last revellers running home. The Festa is over. High up, beyond the Castello and the cappella, the spring among the rocks quickens and swells to a stream. Soon it will be a river, a torrent, a flood.

'Willy, look.'

The note is as pitiful as those prayers for intercession posted to an absent God at the Virgin's hem. Fanny finds it tucked inside the shawl and Jay reads it over William's shoulder.

Dear Mrs Farmer, I expect this will find you because of all the people going to the chapel. You have been ever so kind and I don't know what to do with Mario. When the police came to the camp I ran away because of Sergio. I thought they were looking for us. I will find Sergio and then we'll come back for Mario and go and live somewhere we can be safe. Sorry about the pencil and this writing. Love from Perdita.

'The poor child.'

'What do we do?'

'Sleep,' says William. 'We can't do anything till morning. Mario's got the right idea. We're all worn out.'

Yes, they are tired and it will soon be morning. The holiday is nearly over. The rain pours down and the gutters of the Castello are choked with the litter of the Festa. Lisa comes in late, her dress ripped, soaked, her garland of flowers crushed, to snore till dawn. William gets up once and looks at the sleeping baby. Just a baby. He wonders.

One cannot go on holiday to Italy, simply pick up a baby and take it away. It is not a puppy. It is moreover a child that belongs as much to Italy as to England, even if Italy does not want it.

All this is discussed. Lisa drives to Fiesole for more feeding bottles, formula and disposable nappies (already they have exhausted the Castello's improbable stock).

Jay and Lisa and William talk. It is all, of course, impossible. But something has happened to William, something that has been happening ever since the hornet bite, the sojourn at Daisy's villa, and the search for Fanny. Somehow he has been stung into life and while he nods and agrees with Jay and Lisa, he watches Fanny and would, if he could, have given her Mario. He has put aside his books and some of his fears. He watches her with the baby in the autumn sunshine: a tremulous light. Rain will come again. The trickle of water through the wood has become a bounding stream.

Meanwhile there is Fanny sitting in an upper garden with Mario on a waterproof rug at her feet. She has removed herself from the world of decisions as if the holiday will never be over. It is too late for any mail to reach England before they themselves have returned but all the same she sits in the garden and, taking her pen from her bag and the postcard of the Forli Annunciation, writes to Alison and Rob. It is important to send messages. One must keep on sending.

Now the Festa is over. Felix wakes after all from his wild sleep. He will not die yet, but he has had a scare. His shanks tremble as he gets out of bed, reaches for his spectacles and makes his way to the medicine cabinet. His hand shakes as he makes coffee on the little stove. He opens a window. The weather is bright, but the smell from the garbage is more than usually unpleasant. Ada? No, she is not there and never will be again, in Fra Angelico or anywhere on earth. No angels. No Ada. Just Felix and his heart. He speaks to his wonky friend pumping a little more steadily now: You and I. Hush. Be still. Silence.

And since the Festa the Jackanory girls who had run in the Corsa and danced by the bonfire and painted their nails black and their nipples green and been up to heaven-knows-what in the wood, and got soaked, have come down with colds and drift around miserably sneezing, red-nosed nymphs out of season.

Mario sneezes, astonishing himself. Great joke. He grins at Fanny.

And since the Festa was over the consequences of the absence of the Marchese have become apparent. No one is in control of the Castello. No one has told the workmen to clear up the streets so the litter has not been cleared. No one has put through Fabrizio's order for meat so the meat van from Florence has not arrived. The smell from the garbage heap has become a scandal, the much-anticipated Fellini festival in the cinema is not happening, the bar is running out of vermouth and for some reason no one can explain the tap-water is an unpleasant rusty colour. Ock! says Mrs Peg. She has found a frog in her lavatory.

Fanny baths Mario in a plastic bowl. First she boils the rust-coloured water. Mario loves his bath.

After the Festa and the Marchese's arrest you might have expected Ferdinando to take over. Is he not, after all, rumoured to be an illegitimate sprig of the Marchese's? (Balls, Lisa says, he made that up himself.) But with the Festa done Ferdinando has collapsed. There is no one to tell him what to do. He has had his finest hour. There is nothing left to announce on the public address system. Something has happened to him. He does not bother to shave or to shower. He slumps behind his reception desk in woeful contemplation of a shiny brochure on the Florida Everglades. To enquirers and complainants wanting information about the rusty tap-water, the filthy streets, the stink from the garbage dump, the Fellini festival and the next plane from Pisa to France, America, England, Germany and Holland, Ferdinando pretends that he does not understand what they are saying, even in Italian. And why indeed should he, since there seems no prospect that anyone will pay him to understand? How now will he ever see the World Trade Center or Disneyland or the famous New York muggers?

The second day after the Festa they find the address of the British consulate in Florence in William's Blue Guide. Don't tell Fanny. It is as they expected. A passport cannot be issued without a birth certificate. The father is Italian, you say? It is coming to the end of the season. The vice-consul is weary. The child was born in England but how can they possibly produce Perdita's letter? The vice-consul is sympathetic but under the circumstances it is a matter for the Italian authorities. He gives them an address. Italians love babies, you know.

'Willy, love, it's impossible,' says Lisa. 'Fanny will have to understand.'

William nods. This is not a story. This is life – so much more improbable than fiction. Whoever in fiction would go to Italy on holiday and find a baby in a font? Yet since it has happened it is possible, so nothing is impossible, surely? They are in a muddle but courage and love can sort out muddles and Fanny may yet have her baby.

'Oh Willy, if we could!'

'There might be a way.'

It is dusk. Fanny and William are standing on the terrace of Bronzino. A breeze has carried away the smell of the garbage, the walls of the Castello are fairy battlements, the cypress still black soldiers, guarding.

'Italy is beautiful, isn't it.'

*   *   *

Since the Festa it has rained every night but the days have been brilliant. This morning though, they wake to find that it is still raining and the stream from the cairn above the Virgin's chapel has burst its banks. It no longer flows through the wood. Overnight it has switched its path and runs down the main street of the Castello. The drains are blocked and there is no one to order that they be unblocked, so at the bottom of the hill the water rises. What to do? There is no information. Soon Bronzino and Michelangelo will be an island. William squelches down to the gatehouse. Everyone else has had the same idea and there is chaos in reception. No Ferdinando, so they ask each other: the water is rising, will there be a flood? How do we work the telephone switchboard? How do we confirm our flight reservations? How do we order a car? A taxi to Fiesole? Where is the ten o'clock coach to Florence?

Giotto looks closed up so Miss Stimpson and Miss Head must already have left. William smiles. He imagines them in their Wellington boots and capes wading down the hill to Fiesole. He remembers the view they gave him where there were no violets and Miss Stimpson looked like a girl in her wavy-brimmed sunhat. That seems to have happened a long time ago, it is as distant and yet as sharp in his mind as a childhood picnic. He turns up his collar. He would have liked to say goodbye. He looks up at the sky. What was it Miss Head always said? Saints preserve us.

By midday the exodus has begun. There goes the film director with his nymphs in their slip-slop sandals trailing behind, down to the Lancia in the miraculously unflooded car-park. And Mr and Mrs Peg, sensibly mackintoshed, with one brown fibre suitcase between them. Half an hour ago Felix noticed garbage floating past his window. Only for a second he was tempted to stay put and endure whatever fate was being handed out, but after all he selected those of his belongings he could get into the smaller case and leaving Fra Angelico by the higher back door, skirted the rubbish heap from above and made his way down. He has never seen such rain. Even the last downpour was nothing like this. He can hardly see. He blinks. Isn't that Fanny Farmer with a bundle that looks like a baby? Then he is blind again. He pants, nearly slips, regains his balance and raises his face to the black sky. In what way have we offended thee, oh Lord?

Fanny too looks back. Jay holds an umbrella over her head and she carries the baby wrapped in the grey knitted blanket and William's pack-a-mac. In Florence they will decide what is to be done with Mario. Everything will be settled in Florence. She still has wild hopes she has confided to no one. She looks up in the direction of Santa Maria del Castello and thinks of the rain falling on the small graves, of the spring, the primal source, which appears now to be punishing them. William takes her elbow. Come on, Fan.

No one can speak. Water fills their mouths, their eyes, their ears. So there is no one to hear the public address system crackle waterly. Ferdinando might be speaking from beneath the sea: 'Attenzione! Avvertimento! Alluvione!'

Deaf to this last trump they are settled safely in the Audi, windows up, air-conditioning on, Jay at the wheel. It will be a tricky drive but this is a good weather-car, the Audi will look after them. Look, isn't that Felix getting in his car? We should have thought of him. The Audi breasts confidently the tricky corners and the road which is now more of a river. They pass every other car. At least in this weather no one will be coming up. Jay snaps on the radio. Somewhere else in Italy they are playing football where the sun shines and the ground is hard. They are through Fiesole, approaching the gates of the Villa Inglese, when William takes Fanny's hand and they smile at Mario, sleeping. They do not see the minibus carrying the Japanese up the hill from the European University in search of Dante. Lisa is rummaging in her toy-bag. She brings out the awful Madonna she bought at the market in Fiesole. 'This damn doll.'

As the Audi and the minibus collide head-on there is a moment in which time is suspended, as though eternity had snatched this moment and held it frozen – the minibus skidding, the two vehicles meeting head-on, the spray of water thrown up blinding both drivers, the Japanese covering their eyes with their small paws, Mario sliding from Fanny's lap while Lisa says: this damn doll.

TWELVE

After take-off everyone feels better. That is the worst time when seat-belts are fastened and smoking is forbidden, feeling the aircraft in unnatural labour against air – an element they cannot even see.

Someone asks for a whisky, an English paper, but the cabin staff (who have already flown once today to Heathrow and back again) shake their heads, shrug. They seem faintly contemptuous of their charges. An Italian newspaper, creased, is finally produced but there is no drinks trolley on this short cut-price flight. (The stewardess has reason to be disgruntled. Today should have been her stop-over on a long-haul flight to New York, cancelled because of a bomb threat. She likes America. She sleeps only with American pilots.)

There are no familiar faces. Because of the accident and the delay at Ficsole and then Florence, the Farmers, Jay and Lisa are several days late returning. There is a nun but it is not their nun. There is a couple of elderly Englishwomen, who might be sisters, sharing a thermos of tea, but Miss Stimpson and Miss Head took their flight as booked several days ago. There is a Jewish historian, who could have been Felix Wanderman since Felix on an impulse sold his beetle car in Florence and decided to fly. But that was yesterday. Obviously, there is no Perdita in patched jeans with a baby in a kangaroo pouch.

From the window Fanny has a last sight of Tuscany restored after the flood to a travel poster. The sky is postcard blue. The air is crisp and still. The leaves are burned gold ready to fall. After the rain the olives will be fat. Fanny feels William beside her. She cannot cry.

They are in cloud. William opens his well-thumbed Forster,

closes it and pushes it into the seat-pocket along with the sick-bag,
the emergency instructions and the in-flight magazine. It would
be consoling – simplifying at least – to interpret life through art
and to mourn Mario, like Gino's son on the wild flight from
Monteriano, as a victim of an assortment of muddled motives.
But what happened at the gates of the Villa Inglese was no more
and no less than an accident. William still believes, he insists on
believing, that courage and love might have sorted things out,
but the road was slippery and who could be blamed for the fact
that when Lisa said this damn doll, Jay turned his head for a
moment from the road and the minibus took the corner a
little close and the two vehicles collided? Accidents come from
nowhere and mean nothing. That is a bleak fact. William closes
his eyes and faces it.

And yet, thinks Fanny. And yet it would be easier to conclude
that someone is always responsible for the small unmarked body
stacked in the morgue at Florence pending enquiries. If she had
not tried to save him Mario might not have been lost. Someone
else might have found him in the font. But if you think like that
in the end the chain of responsibility brings you up against a
nonsense: if Mario had not been born he would not have died.
(If Sebastian had not been conceived he would not have died in
her womb.)

What in any case had she intended to do with Mario? At the
time she had thought, simply to love. She remembers the
wonderful dream of the lily and the rose. She looks across at
Jay (who loves her) and remembers all the red roses. Perhaps
she says aloud and possibly William hears her: We were only
pretending, weren't we?

Lisa (who has caught a baby in Italy, as her mother would
say, and has at this moment decided to keep it) reaches across
the gangway to pass the creased Italian newspaper. It is folded
back at the second page. Lisa points to a paragraph near the
bottom. The hijack is old news. Sergio Dolci, it appears, has
disappeared, he is perduto to the polizia. Fanny looks out. There
might be no earth beneath that cloud but there is and somewhere
in a secret world on the old, round, desperate planet, Perdita
will find her Sergio and they will live, somehow.

A gap in the cloud reveals a rain-soaked Sunday England. At last Fanny begins to weep, not wildly but steadily, penitently and gratefully, as though she could already feel that kind rain on her face.

They are going down. Rosary time again. It is raining in England, their captain says. At the moment of descent as they bumpily surrender their battle with gravity, the captain receives a message from Pisa. General alert at all airports. A bomb has been planted. Bomba. It could be a hoax.

As the plane banks it seems to the passengers as if the earth itself had tipped on its axis, might flip off into space.

GORDON LISH

DEAR MR. CAPOTE

David is a seemingly ordinary middle-aged bank clerk and conscientious father living in New York. Until he starts writing letters to author Truman Capote, proposing to kill forty-seven women for his forty-seven years and offering these memoirs to Capote as a possible financial deal. Brilliantly, Lish immerses us in the extraordinary mind of a murderer and madman. A searingly realistic portrayal from an original fictional voice, DEAR MR. CAPOTE demands comparison with IN COLD BLOOD and THE EXECUTIONER'S SONG.

'One of the best first novels of the year . . . A real grabber . . . strikingly original'
New York Times Book Review

'Subtle and profound, dreadful and wonderful'
Stanley Ellin in the Washington Post

'Who else has shaped the shapelessness of madness with such horrific artistry?'
Cynthia Ozick, author of LEVITATIONS

sceptre

NAYANTARA SAHGAL

RICH LIKE US

A story of India: the recent India of Mrs Gandhi's Emergency when power became arbitrary once more, when – as always in such times – the corrupt, the opportunist and the bully flourished.

A story also of an older India, of a generation who remember the British Raj and Partition, of the continuities and the ties of family and caste and religion that stretch back and back.

But above all, and memorably, it is a story of people: of Rose, the Cockney memsahib, of Western-educated Sonali and traditionally brought-up Mona, of Ravi, Marxist turned placeman, and Kishori Lal, the old idealist who finds that once again a man can be imprisoned just for what he thinks.

'Funny, readable and startlingly intelligent'
The Listener

'A fascinating book to read, from first to last'
London Magazine

'Dry and sardonic . . . subtle, powerful'
New Statesman

sceptre

IRMGARD KEUN

AFTER MIDNIGHT

'And now I feel like crying, because I really do *not* understand, and I don't think I will when I'm older, either'

Nineteen-year-old Susanne is not political. She is an ordinary, fairly carefree teenager who lives with her brother Algin, a writer. But her life is increasingly disrupted by the pressures of the Nazi regime. Queues of people form as informers flock to denounce their neighbours. Someone has invented a divining rod to detect Jews. Algin's books are banned and finally her boyfriend is arrested for 'talking like a communist'.

First published in 1937 in Amsterdam, and written in the natural, often surprisingly humorous, prose of a young girl, AFTER MIDNIGHT paints a terrifying picture of Germany under the Third Reich.

'I cannot think of anything else that conjures up so powerfully the atmosphere of a nation turned insane . . . one of those pieces of fiction that illuminate fact'
Sunday Telegraph

sceptre

MELVYN BRAGG

THE CUMBRIAN TRILOGY

Melvyn Bragg's celebrated trilogy – THE HIRED MAN,
A PLACE IN ENGLAND and KINGDOM COME – traces
four generations of Tallentire history: from John in the rural
Cumbria of 1898 to Douglas in the competitive and back-
biting metropolis of the Seventies. From 'hired man' to
media man worlds have been bridged, but the old ideals of
success, freedom and happiness seem ever elusive as each
Tallentire must come to terms with private uncertainty and
pain.

'An uncommonly high talent. The people are "real" enough to
leave footprints right across the page'
The Guardian

'A novelist of power and imagination. It is one of Bragg's gifts
to create his own atmosphere and so heighten feeling'
New Society

sceptre

Current and forthcoming titles from Sceptre

GORDON LISH

DEAR MR. CAPOTE

NAYANTARA SAHGAL

RICH LIKE US

IRMGARD KEUN

AFTER MIDNIGHT

MELVYN BRAGG

THE CUMBRIAN TRILOGY

MARK CHILDRESS

A WORLD MADE OF FIRE

BOOKS OF DISTINCTION

sceptre